DEEP WATERS

SEA OF MERMAID SECRETS

 1

USA TODAY BESTSELLING AUTHOR

ALICIA RADES

SEA OF MERMAID SECRETS SERIES

Deep Waters
Rising Tides
Crashing Waves

ALSO BY ALICIA RADES

HIDDEN LEGENDS: ACADEMY OF MAGICAL CREATURES

The Fire Prophecy

The Water Legacy

The Earth Legend

The Air Omen

The Elemental War

The Soul Sacrifice

HIDDEN LEGENDS: COLLEGE OF WITCHCRAFT

The Coven's Secret

The Reaper's Shadow

The Cauldron's Curse

The Demon's Spell

The Warlock's Trial

The Witch's Fate

HIDDEN LEGENDS: PRISON FOR SUPERNATURAL OFFENDERS

The Villain Institute

The Criminal Lair

The Infernal Underground

The Assassin's Destiny

The Devil's City

The Elven Gate

Vengeance and Vampires

Ravenite

Resilience

Resolute

Retribute

Crystal Frost

Fire in Frost

Desire in Frost

Inspired by Frost

Fading Frost

Davina Universe

Divine Fate Trilogy:

Chosen by Grace

Touched by Grace

Awakened by Grace

Divine Descendants Duology:

Concealing Magic

Exposing Magic

CHAPTER 1

Thunder cracked outside my window, startling me awake for the third time that night. I groaned and folded the pillow over my head. All I wanted to do was sleep. Clearly, that wasn't in the cards tonight.

Another crack of thunder reverberated throughout the house. The crystals hanging from my lamp shade jingled together. Then, just like that, the rain pelting against my window slowed to a light, quiet drizzle. The lightning vanished as if someone turned off the switch to a strobe light.

I breathed a sigh of relief. I wasn't entirely sure I'd slept at all in the last two hours.

Though I welcomed the quiet, I couldn't bring myself to fall asleep. By the time the rain completely stopped tapping against my window, I was still staring hopelessly across the room at my dresser, where my shell collection and jars of sand art sat. At some point, the clouds cleared, and the moonlight shone in through my window to illuminate the silhouettes of my furniture.

The small analog clock on my nightstand ticked in my ear, reminding me of the minutes I'd been lying awake. It was almost worse than the thunder. *Almost.*

I didn't know how long it'd been, but eventually, I caved to the mocking tick of my clock. I tossed the covers off my body and swung my legs over the side of the bed. Sleep wasn't coming, and lying there praying it would wasn't going to help anything. I needed to take a break and try again later.

I tiptoed around a stack of textbooks and the laundry basket full of stuff Mom had bought me for my dorm room. I was moving into the dorms next week and hadn't started packing yet. It wasn't like I couldn't come home if I forgot something, though. The school was just on the other side of town.

I snuck out of my bedroom. On my way to the back door, I peeked into my parents' room. Their still bodies and quiet breathing indicated that they'd somehow slept through the storm.

I didn't bother with shoes as I tiptoed out of the house

and down to the sandy beach that came up to touch the back patio. I always went barefoot on my late-night walks when I couldn't sleep. The wet sand squished between my toes, relieving some of the tension in my shoulders. I inhaled a deep breath, which felt heavy in my lungs after the rain, but the salty scent of the ocean calmed me even more. My white nightgown danced in the light breeze, and the only sound I could hear was the ocean waves softly lapping over the shore.

Cool water rushed over my toes. I wiggled my fingers, and tiny beads of water rose into the air at my command. I smiled as I let the droplets rain back into the ocean. It was when I was one with the water that I felt most alive.

The moon shone just bright enough to guide my path. I passed by my neighbors' houses and spotted the pile of rocks that rose from the sea ahead of me. Those rocks marked the public beach up ahead, where teens like me hung out most days.

In Sea Haven, California, we lived for the beach and the ocean. The sea was where we came from. It was part of who we were.

I spotted a rock up ahead and decided I'd turn around once I hit it, then try sleeping again. As I neared the tall rock in front of me, a new figure took shape. I'd been to this beach enough times that I knew every single rock. Anyone could pick up a stone and I'd know if it was out of place. So, what was that lump on shore that wasn't supposed to be there?

Something must've washed ashore in the storm. A clump of seaweed? A dolphin? A treasure chest?

I crept toward the shape carefully. The lump of... whatever it was... was slightly bigger than me. It was longer than it was tall, which almost made it look like a sunbather lying on their back. Actually, the bumps and curves made it look like the shape had a head... and a nose... OH MY GOD!

I rushed the last several yards to the figure and dropped to my knees near his chest. *A person! It's a person!*

I frantically searched for signs of life by pressing my ear to his chest. His heart was still beating, and my relief came out sounding like a small shriek.

Only when I confirmed the man was alive did I pull away to inspect his features. In the moonlight, I saw that he had long hair and a matching beard. My gaze trailed down to his muscled torso. He wasn't wearing a shirt, just a necklace with a blue stone.

I had no idea who he was or how he'd gotten here. I knew everyone in Sea Haven—maybe not by name, but by face. I was born and raised here. It wasn't like anyone came and went from our town—not when we had to hide our magic from the rest of the world.

Maybe he was a sailor who got caught in the storm. When my gaze traveled toward his legs, I nearly toppled over in surprise.

I inhaled an audible breath. "No. Fricking. Way."

The legs I was searching for weren't there. In their place was a fish-like tail with green scales that reflected the moonlight. How hadn't I noticed these beautiful scales from a distance? His tail extended longer than I would have expected. The end split in two directions and lay motionless in the sand while the waves licked the bottom few inches.

I didn't know how long it took me to finally breathe again. Merfolk weren't real—not anymore.

I knew the stories. My people were descended from merfolk, but our ancestors had died out centuries ago. We could still manipulate water to our command, commune with sea life, and breathe under water, but we no longer had tails, and we'd long since lost the supersonic scream and siren call of our ancestors. Everything I'd ever known told me this man shouldn't exist.

I involuntarily reached out and ran my fingers along the merman's scales. They were smoother than I expected. I inspected the area where his scales met his skin, as if I expected to find a seam that would tell me his tail was fake. But his tail and torso blended together so perfectly that there was no mistaking it.

If this was real, if it wasn't some twisted dream or sick joke, then how was it that Sea Haven residents had been led to believe for so long that our ancestors were extinct? I'd always thought we were all that was left of them.

There was no way the Sea Haven Council knew about this. If they did, they would've told us.

I had to tell my dad. He worked at City Hall and knew people on the council. He'd be able to help the merman.

Before I could get to my feet, the man twitched. I froze

just long enough to make sure I wasn't imagining things. His hand twitched again in my direction, and I grabbed it.

"Are you okay?" I asked desperately.

His eyes opened just a sliver, just enough to see I was there. He lifted his opposite hand, and it shook as if he was using all his strength to reach out and touch me. I remained frozen as his cold fingers lightly grazed my cheek. The man forced his eyes open wider. They focused on mine as if he couldn't quite believe what he was seeing, like he wasn't sure I was actually there.

Those blue-green eyes left me speechless. Somehow in the moonlight, they shone brighter than they should. It was as if the magic behind them defined their color, their brightness. They were the color of the ocean, and staring into them felt like home.

My left hand came up to meet his right, which still touched my face. His fingers were icy cold, and for some reason, I felt obligated to warm them for him.

"What's your name?" I whispered.

He spoke in a deep, raspy voice so hoarse I could barely understand him. "Tristan."

"Tristan? I'm Bree."

The corners of his lips twitched as he attempted a smile. I was about to ask him if he was hurt, but before I could, his eyes rolled back into his head, and his hands went limp in mine.

A string of curse words escaped my lips. I sprang to my feet and took off running down the shore. I didn't think I'd ever sprinted so fast in my life. I was in such a hurry that when I flung open the glass door and hurried across the kitchen floor, my wet feet slipped out from under me. My elbow cracked against the tile, but I didn't have time to process the pain or assess the damage. I scrambled to my feet and ran toward my parents' room.

"Dad!" I heaved in his doorway.

No response.

It took three wide steps to make it to his bedside, where I shook him awake. "Dad!"

He blinked a few times and gazed up at me in confusion.

"I need your help. *Now.*"

Noticing my urgency, he sprang up in bed, scooped up his phone from his nightstand, and followed me. He didn't ask any questions. He just raced barefoot out the door with me.

I attempted to fill him in as we hurried back down the shore, but I doubted I was making any sense. I managed to get in a few fragments of the story. "Couldn't sleep. Went for a walk. Merman. Dad, they're real! Needs help. Didn't know what else to do. The council has to know about this."

I didn't slow as I approached Tristan. I only stopped when I dropped to my knees next to him. He remained unresponsive, and that made my racing pulse speed up even faster. Was I too late?

"Tristan." I shook his shoulders. "Tristan, I brought help." My voice cracked out of desperation. I jumped when my father placed his hand on my shoulder.

"Bree," my dad said gently.

The sound of my father's voice eased my anxiety. He guided me away from Tristan. My father took my spot in the sand next to him to inspect for injuries.

"Is he going to be okay?" I demanded.

After confirming that Tristan was still breathing, my father turned to me. "I have to tell the council about this. We have no idea what this could mean for our people. Go home. Don't tell anyone about this, okay? Not even your mother. Merfolk have engaged in war with us before, and we don't want to start a panic until we know more."

"But Dad—" I started.

"He's going to be okay," he promised, resting a hand on my shoulder for reassurance.

I trusted my father wholeheartedly. So when he promised that Tristan would be all right, I believed him. I turned away and headed down the beach.

My father's voice grew distant, carried away by the light breeze. When I glanced back at him, I could just barely make out his outline illuminated by the moonlight. He held his phone to his ear and talked into it. I couldn't make out his words, but there was no way in *hell* I was going to walk away from this.

I snuck behind a rock and watched. I watched as Carson Ray, head of the Sea Haven Council, parked his black sedan next to the beach. I watched as he crossed the sand and knelt next to Tristan and exchanged words with my father, though I couldn't hear what he said. I watched as another vehicle—a van—drove up a few minutes later. I watched as two other men stepped out of it and met my father and Carson next to Tristan. I watched as all four of them hoisted Tristan up and placed him in the back of the dark van.

Chilly night air crept over my skin as I peeked from behind my rock. Carson Ray slammed the back door of the van, then turned to survey the beach. My heart hammered as I ducked behind my rock, pressing my back to it and squeezing my eyes shut tightly. The breeze caught my nightgown, blowing it to the side. I grabbed the hem as quickly as I could and pulled it close to me, praying Carson Ray hadn't seen. I held my breath, until the sounds of tires retreated into the distance.

I peeked back over the rock to find myself alone in the night. I had no choice but to head home. If I wasn't home by the time my father arrived, I'd be entering deep waters.

Somehow, I already knew I was in deep. I couldn't get my father's warning out of my head.

Don't tell anyone about this, okay? Not even your mother.

Those didn't sound like promising words. They sounded like a warning.

CHAPTER 2

"You've got to be kidding me," my best friend Liana insisted the next day.

"I'm dead serious." My eyes widened from where I sat on her bed.

"Christina did *not* say Sam was hotter than Dean." Liana turned back toward her mirror, where she was brushing out her long blond hair.

I held several strands of my own dark hair out in front of my face and absentmindedly picked at the split ends. You'd think with magic running through my veins, I'd be able to mend a few split ends, but I couldn't.

I wonder what Tristan can do, I thought. Legend said our ancestors could control the oceans, but after they settled in Sea Haven and began mating with humans, their magic grew weaker with every generation, until our people sealed off the town. No one came in. No one came out.

Okay, that wasn't completely true. We had suppliers and contractors who came and went, but we tried our best to remain as self-sustaining as possible. That's why there was a small university in town with a select few graduate programs so that some of us could learn to become doctors and stuff instead of having to reveal the secret of our magic.

And it's not like no one *ever* left. There was a guy a grade ahead of me, Noah Starr, who left for school outside of Sea Haven last year. It's not like we *can't* leave. We just don't want to. Keeping to ourselves and not welcoming outsiders was what was going to preserve the last bits of magic we had left.

Our magic was everything to our people. Our economy was built on the exportation of fish and other seafood, and we used our magic to maintain marine populations and ocean health. Our favorite pastimes were on the water—fishing, surfing, boating, swimming. Every year, Sea Haven put on Sea Festival, a three-day sporting event with swimming competitions, fishing derbies, surfing tournaments, and the best seafood on the coast. Everything we did came back to the water.

"Bree," Liana called. "Are you even listening to me?"

"Huh?" I raised my brows and let my split ends fall

back to my chest. "Yeah, I'm listening. Dean is hotter, hands down. But I mean, come on. You can't say Sam *isn't* hot."

"Oh, sure. I mean, they're brothers. They share the same DNA."

I looked at her sideways. "You *do* know they're actors, right? We may be freaks of nature, but *Supernatural* is fiction, Li."

She rolled her eyes and turned to me, leaning her arm up against the back of her chair. "You know what I meant. But we're agreed, then? Dean is the hottest guy we know?"

I sighed. *Tristan sure could give Dean a run for his money.*

Tristan.

The thought echoed through my mind. I'd only met him last night, but already, the whole thing was starting to feel like a dream. Only, since I'd lain awake the entire rest of the night, I knew I hadn't dreamt it.

I wanted to tell Liana about him. I'd already almost blurted it out a couple of times. But my dad had warned me not to mention anything, and until I could get more answers out of him, I was keeping my mouth shut. I didn't want to put Liana in any danger.

I'd wanted to ask my dad about it this morning, but when I finally pulled myself out of bed after struggling for hours for a lick of sleep, he was already gone.

He'd told me to pretend like nothing happened, and so I did.

But all I could do was *pretend*. That didn't keep the reality of the situation from burrowing itself into my mind, taking up a home in every thought of mine. Our ancestors were out there.

"Bree," Liana complained again, pulling me out of my thoughts again.

"Yes," I said. "Dean is the hottest guy we know. Though technically we don't really *know* him."

In one swift move, Liana leapt from her chair and pulled the pillow I'd been leaning against out from under me. She aimed an attack straight at my face, but I dodged it, nearly toppling off her bed.

"Don't you ever say he's just a fictional character!" she shouted playfully. "You're ruining all the fun."

She took another swat at me, but I quickly sank off the edge of the bed and onto the floor.

"You're going to have to be faster than that if you're going to catch *this* girl," I snickered.

She jumped onto the bed and aimed the pillow at my face. I rolled across the carpet just as the pillow made contact with the floor right where my head lay a split second ago.

"You're as slow as a sea horse," I teased.

"Gah!" She shrieked and grabbed the pillow again to take another shot at me. "Stop calling me a sea horse."

She gritted her teeth, and I smiled in triumph as I dodged yet another one of her blows. I raced to the other side of the room, but she now had two pillows in her hands.

I glanced around in search of my own weapon, but as soon as my gaze fell upon the ocean outside her window, the fight we were having suddenly didn't matter anymore. I froze in front of the window, staring out at the waves. My memories flickered back to the previous night, first to Tristan's green scales, then to the blue-green color of his eyes, and then to my father telling me to go back home. To tell no one what I saw.

Something hard smacked into the right side of my face. It was so unexpected that I tumbled to the ground. I caught myself with the palms of my hands. When I looked up to see what had happened, I found Liana standing above me, her jaw hanging open.

"I'm *so* sorry. I didn't mean to hit you so hard. Are you okay?" She dropped the pillows to her feet and offered her hand to help me up.

I grumbled but took her hand anyway. "Yeah, I'm fine."

"What were you looking at?" She narrowed her eyes out the window, searching for anything out of the ordinary.

I shrugged. "Just the ocean."

She sighed softly. "It looks so peaceful out there." Her tone quickly became more upbeat. "Hey, want to go for a swim?"

My heart lifted. A swim was exactly what I needed. "Absolutely."

Liana slipped into her swimming suit and had her beach bag packed within minutes. We made the short walk down the sand to my house, where I dressed in my own swimsuit and packed up my towel.

Liana inhaled a deep breath as we stepped out my back door. "It's such a nice day today."

She spread her arms wide as if that would help her soak up the sun.

"It's been a nice summer," I remarked.

Liana kept her eyes on the crowded beach ahead. "Except last night. Did that big crack of thunder wake you up?"

"*That big crack of thunder?*" I repeated. "You mean the two-hundred cracks of thunder?"

I thought back to Tristan, how I'd walked this same path last night only to find him on the beach in front of me. It almost didn't seem like the same place. Last night, it was so quiet, so secluded. Now I could hardly see the sand through the crowd, and I could hear the laughter all the way from my house. It almost had me questioning if it all had been real.

Almost.

Liana shrugged. "I'm kind of looking forward to the summer being over. I'm excited about college. Living with you in the dorms will be fun, don't you think?"

I nodded.

Liana and I were going to be roommates. She was majoring in psychology, though I was still undecided. My parents and teachers always said I had *potential*, but I was only eighteen. I needed more time to figure out who I was before I decided what I wanted to do with the rest of my life.

"I'm excited, but I'm *so* not ready for the summer to be over," I said.

"Well..." She dragged out the word and wiggled her eyebrows at me. "We still have a week left. Let's make the most of it. Race you!"

Liana took off sprinting toward the beach.

"Not fair!" I called after her, running just fast enough that she maintained a fair distance ahead. After calling her a sea horse earlier, I supposed I could spare her a win in the speed department.

Liana hit the swimming area first. She dropped her beach bag to the sand and raced toward the water, not wasting a second to dive into it. I followed right behind, tossing my bag next to hers and hitting the water a moment later. I splashed her as soon as she stood.

"Hey." She retaliated.

The cold salt water felt refreshing on my skin.

Without saying another word, Liana disappeared under the water. I followed. Under water, it was an entirely different world. Everyone was off for summer vacation, which meant that children, teens, and young adults of all ages were swimming today. Since Sea Haven Beach was the best spot in the area for a swim, I couldn't look anywhere without seeing a swarm of people. Right, left. Up, down. It didn't matter.

I inhaled the salty water. It was like a breath of fresh air, like somehow I wasn't breathing properly until now.

Liana kicked in front of me, sending bubbles in her wake. I followed the trail until we found an open area at the edge of the crowd. She claimed the spot by flipping over and summersaulting backward. I joined her with a front summersault. She gave me a thumbs-up and then signaled to a rock a good forty yards away.

I kicked off the ocean floor. Water swished by my foot as she attempted to reach out for my ankle to slow me down, but she didn't manage it. I commanded a stream of water to push me forward, and I tagged the rock before she could grab my foot.

She narrowed her eyes at me playfully. I smiled back in triumph.

Liana and I spent hours in the water. We started close to shore and let the rip tide take us far away, before swimming back to shallow waters and riding the current all over again. Then we dove under water looking for shells and saved a few on a reef that we'd come back for later.

An orange fish swam by me, making circles around my feet and tickling my toes before moving on. I spotted a large lobster with no claws and long red streaks along its legs hiding in a crevice of the rock. Liana pointed out a black rockfish, then picked up a mollusk with a beautiful shiny purple and green shell. I ran a finger over his shell, using my magic to soothe the creature. His emotions poured into me, and I felt his initial shock subside.

I couldn't *speak* with the marine life, but my strong connection told me what they were feeling.

I caught sight of something yellow, and I tapped Liana on the shoulder. Her eyes lit up when she saw the sunflower star, a starfish-like creature with over twenty limbs.

Liana pointed to the surface. We could only stay under water for a few hours until we had to resurface for air. We left the sea life behind, and I kicked my feet until my head broke the water. I pushed the hair from my face and wiped the water from my eyes.

"Look!" Liana pointed toward the horizon, and I spotted a pod of dolphins leaping into the air.

A grin spread across my face. "Race you!"

Liana ducked under water again, but I went for the surface. Magic coursed through my veins as I manipulated the water to my command. Water swirled around my legs, and a wave pushed me upward, until only my feet were submerged. I ordered the water to carry me out to sea.

I funneled more magic into the wave, until it carried me higher and higher. The wave peaked twenty feet above the surface of the ocean before I grew tired.

A dolphin poked her head out of the water and gave me a few happy clicks. The wave I rode settled, and I sank into the water again.

I reached for the dolphin and gently ran my hand across the top of her head. "Hey, Delphina."

Delphina nuzzled into me. I'd met Delphina when I was a kid, and we'd grown up together. I often brought her fish, and she liked bringing me shiny shells she'd found. Next to Liana and Christina, this dolphin was one of my best friends.

"Want to go for a swim?" I asked.

Delphina threw her head back, and I felt her excitement surge through me.

"You better hurry up, or I'm leaving without you," Liana teased. I turned to see she was already on the back of a dolphin. She'd beat me to them.

"Let's go," I told Delphina. I flattened myself against her body and held on tight to her dorsal fin. The dolphin flipped her tail, and we took off.

Laughter filled the air as Liana and I rode the dolphins through the water. They jumped, leaping into the air before diving back down again. Bubbles tickled my skin as we moved through the water faster than I could swim on my own. I never felt more free than I did when I was in the water. Here, my heart was full.

The dolphins swam around a boat, and we waved to the fishermen aboard. One of the fishermen blew into a conch shell, and the dolphins clicked happily in response.

The dolphins swam us back to shore, and we waved goodbye as they swam away. Liana and I climbed the rocks to the tide pools, and I plopped down next to a pool of sea urchins and anemones. I drew in a deep, refreshing breath as my eyes took in the beautiful blues and teals of the ocean.

I turned my gaze to the old lighthouse that stood on an outcropping of rock down the beach. It was one of my favorite places in all of Sea Haven. It had been decommissioned years ago, but it was so picturesque against the shoreline.

"I love the ocean," Liana said as she leaned back on the rock beside me.

I turned my head up toward the sun. "It never gets old."

"Never," Liana sighed happily.

No truer words had ever been spoken. There were new things to discover all the time. Green scales dominated my thoughts. I found myself scanning the ocean as far out as I could see, almost like I expected to see more merfolk follow Tristan to Sea Haven. He wasn't even supposed to be alive, so where did he come from?

After minutes of silence, Liana propped herself up on her elbows. "I'm getting really hungry. Do you want get some food?"

Only then did I realize how hungry I'd become. "Sure. My mom made salmon pasta last night if you want to do leftovers."

"I love your mom's pasta!" she exclaimed.

At the beach, we scooped up our bags and wrapped our towels around ourselves. Liana discussed her ideas for decorating our dorm room on the way back, but I didn't process much of it. My attention remained locked on the horizon.

When we entered the back door, I was shocked to find my father sitting at the kitchen table. "Dad, you're home. Why aren't you at work?"

"Hi, Mr. Waters," Liana greeted.

My father folded his newspaper and gazed up at me past his reading glasses. His graying hair appeared unkempt, which made him look grouchy. "I took a half day."

"Okay." I crossed around the counter and opened the fridge. I did my best to keep my voice even, but my dad only ever took off work when he was sick. What could it mean that he was sitting at home in the middle of the day on a Friday? He didn't *look* sick—just grumpy.

"Liana and I were going to have leftovers. Want me to heat some up for you?" I asked.

"No." He cleared his throat. "After you two are done eating, I'd like your help with something, Bree."

I closed the fridge, the container of leftovers in my hand. "Can I help you later? We're going to head back down to the beach when we're done eating."

"I need your help while I'm off work," he pressed.

"Okay..." Somehow, I knew this wasn't going to be good.

I ate slowly, stalling whatever it was my father needed me for. I didn't want to be alone with him. He'd just go on pretending like nothing happened, and I'd be sitting here anxiously wanting to ask him about it.

But I couldn't stop the inevitable from happening.

"I'll see you later," Liana said after setting her dishes in the sink. "I'll be down at the beach whenever you're done if you want to hang out."

"Okay." I waved. "See you later."

As soon as the back door slid shut, I whirled toward my father. Whatever he needed help with better be good. "What's going on?"

"Why don't you go change?" he suggested, gesturing toward my swimming suit.

I planted my feet on the tile floor. "First, tell me what this is about."

I knew I came off sounding rude, but after what happened last night, I couldn't help it.

My father stood and cleared his throat. "The council wants to see you."

CHAPTER 3

My mind raced the whole ride to City Hall. Were they going to tell me the truth? Had they known our ancestors were still out there?

Calm down, Bree, I told myself. *This may not be about Tristan at all.*

Except, I knew it was. No one could discover something so amazing and expect to go on living like nothing ever happened.

After he parked the car, my father turned to me. I spoke before he had a chance. "This is about Tristan, isn't it?"

"I think you need to hear what the council has to say."

"Did they know he existed?" I demanded.

He shook his head. "The council is as shocked as we are. They want to talk to you."

"Fine, but I need answers!"

Dad pressed his fingers to his eyes. "I don't have all the answers. I'm not on the council, Bree. I'm just a paper pusher. What I know is that what you found is incredibly dangerous—"

"*What I found?*" I repeated. "Dad, that man is a living person! Am I in trouble?"

"No, honey." His voice cracked. I didn't understand why he was acting so emotional. His words seemed innocent enough, but the tears in his eyes told me there was more to it than that. "But everything's going to be all right."

We exited the car and walked up the stairs side by side, but neither of us said anything. The cool air inside the building hit me when we stepped through the doors. It was like walking through a portal to another climate. A woman's heels clicked against the tile, echoing down the hall. I glanced down at my sandals, wondering if I was underdressed.

"This way." My father gestured for me to follow him.

We took a turn down the hall to our left. He stopped at the door on the end and knocked.

"Come in." I recognized Carson Ray's voice. He was head of the Sea Haven Council and my father's boss.

My father opened the door but stepped aside so I

could enter first. Hues of brown bathed the wide room. The walls were wood grain a few shades darker than the hardwood floor, and matching bookshelves stood along the right side of the room. Two leather chairs were situated in front of Carson's desk. The chair behind his desk had a taller back and swiveled when he stood. A small tabletop fountain sat on the wide windowsill behind his desk between two jade plants. It filled the room with the trickling sound of water that perhaps would have helped ease my nerves if I didn't feel like I was walking into a courtroom.

I plastered a fake smile on my face. Maybe there was still hope that this meeting wasn't bad news.

"Hello," I greeted kindly. The obvious fakeness to it made me want to puke, but neither Carson nor my father seemed to notice. I shook Carson's outstretched hand.

"Please, have a seat." He gestured to the two chairs opposite his desk.

My father and I sat. After a moment, I noticed how tightly I was gripping the arm of the chair. I placed my hands in my lap, forcing myself to relax.

Carson straightened his tie as his sat. "Miss Waters."

"Bree," I corrected.

"Bree." Carson said my name slowly. "I asked you and your father to meet me here today because I have some good news for you."

If it was good news, why had my father been crying earlier? I looked to him for an explanation, but he kept his gaze locked ahead on Carson. I wasn't sure how he managed that considering the bald spot atop Carson's head was practically blinding.

"Good news?" I asked.

"Yes." He smiled. "My wife put in a recommendation for you at a college that has an excellent journalism program."

I furrowed my brow. "Mrs. Ray? My English teacher?"

I found that hard to believe considering she didn't even *like* me. On my final paper senior year, one of her comments read, "Lacks depth and creativity." I think she had a thing against me ever since I came to her class the first day of school chewing gum. And then there was that time I pointed out her error on the board in using *your* instead of *you're*. And that other time when... yeah, okay. Mrs. Ray had plenty of reasons not to like me.

Carson nodded, his smile not wavering.

"What makes her think I want to go into journalism?" The idea of being a journalist made me want to gag.

Carson's smile faded. He quickly flipped through the stack of papers on his desk until he found what he was looking for three pages down. "Her recommendation here says you were one of the best writers in her class. She told me personally that you wrote several inspiring poems during your poetry unit."

The confusion in my expression deepened, and I spoke slowly. "Yeah, but that's poetry, not journalism. I don't get it. Why are you the one telling me this?"

Carson folded his hands across the stack of papers in

front of him. "My wife is very busy this week, so she asked me to deliver the news personally. We're very proud of you, Miss Waters."

This was all so confusing that I could hardly get the words out. "You're... proud that... I wrote some good poems in high school?"

When Carson laughed, his whole chair shook. "We're proud that you have the opportunity to attend such a wonderful college."

I narrowed my eyes, trying my best to look past him so I wouldn't go blind looking at his shiny bald head. I thought I was coming in here to answer questions about last night, about Tristan. What did any of this have to do with him?

I forced my voice to remain strong. "I'm going to school in Sea Haven, just like everyone else."

"No, honey." I was surprised to hear my father speak for the first time since we walked into Carson's office.

My gaze fell on him. The look in his eyes said it all. They were sending me away because of what I saw. They were trying to cover it up. But... why?

Was my father one of the bad guys?

I didn't believe that for a second. My father was good through and through. But that didn't mean he wasn't working for the bad guys.

I looked back to Carson, my nostrils flaring. "So, I got into another college just like that?" I snapped my fingers. My words spilled out of my mouth quickly, as if I could somehow reason with him about how much this didn't make any sense. "I didn't even apply! It's only a week until classes start. Application periods are over. How could I have gotten in on such short notice?"

Carson shrugged like he wasn't sure how it happened, but he smiled like it was a happy accident. "The school was very impressed by the recommendation my wife sent in."

Suddenly, I couldn't breathe. I gripped the ends of the armrests again until my knuckles turned white. My breath grew hot, making it feel like I was breathing fire onto my upper lip. The water in the small fountain behind Carson's desk began to drip at an irregular rate.

They're going to kill me for what I know! They're going to tell everyone I went off to journalism school, and they're going to kill me! Is that what happened to everyone else who left? Was it because they saw something they shouldn't have?

"Where is this *school*?" I couldn't keep the sarcastic tone out of my voice when I said the word *school*. There probably wasn't one. It was all just a ruse to shut me up, to lock me in a jail cell or smother me in my sleep.

Carson handed the top paper on his stack over to me. I leaned forward in my chair and snatched it out of his hands. It took me a second to find mention of the location, but when I did, I shot out of my chair. The water in his fountain began a reverse course. I was kind of scared for my life here; I couldn't exactly help it.

"*Illinois!*" I exclaimed so loud that I was sure I heard the word echo down the hall despite the door being closed.

My father reached out for me to get me to settle down, but I shrugged him off. Carson's smile completely faded, but I could have sworn he looked *amused* by my outburst.

"That's in the middle of the country! The ocean! I—I need to be by..." My words trailed off as I collapsed back into my chair. *The ocean doesn't matter when you're dead.*

"Bree, honey—" my dad tried, but I cut him off.

"No." I straightened in my chair and looked Carson Ray dead in the eyes. "Why don't we talk about what this is really about?"

My eyebrow twitched, challenging him.

"It's just about your academics, Miss Waters," he replied calmly.

My eye twitched this time. Woops. I didn't mean to do that. "Really? So you don't want to ask me any questions about a certain someone I met last night?"

Carson swallowed hard, and my father's breathing rate increased.

Dad sighed. "Carson, we can't act like it never happened. You have to tell my daughter the truth. We had a deal."

Carson pursed his lips. "I did not want to frighten her, but very well. What you discovered last night is deeply troubling. Evidence that merfolk still exist threatens our very existence."

"Why?" I asked. "We're descended from them. We share their blood."

"You don't know what they're capable of," Carson insisted. "Full-blooded merfolk have powers beyond your capabilities. This merman can brew storms bigger than the sea that could take out our whole town. He still has his siren song. He has the power of compulsion, and he's already made it clear that he wants to compel *you*."

"Me?" I balked.

"You're the one who found him, and he's taken a particular interest in you," Carson said. "This is why we must send you away—for your protection."

I looked to my dad in disbelief. "You agreed to this?"

"I agreed to protect you," Dad promised. "We can't release the merman, not until we've learned what he knows. There could be others coming. In the meantime, I want to keep you safe."

Carson leaned forward. "You must not tell anyone of what you've seen, or it will put your friends and family in danger. We have things under control for the time being, but we must keep this quiet. Believe me, it's best for everyone. I suggest you take the rest of the afternoon to pack your bags and say goodbye. We'll need you back here by nine o'clock tonight to make final preparations. Your flight leaves quite early in the morning. We'll have a car ready for you with your itinerary and class schedule."

"You can't send me away," I begged.

Carson stood, pressing his palms firmly to the table and leaning over to stare me straight in the eyes. "This is what must be done. You will be leaving, and you will leave without telling anyone the reason."

He stood up straight and adjusted his tie. "I trust you

can find a way to explain this to your friends and family without divulging too many *details*."

Explain it to my friends and family? How could I ever explain this? You're taking my life from me! You ARE the bad guy! I wanted to shout it all at him, but all the air had left my lungs, and I couldn't find my tongue.

Somehow, my father managed to pull me up from my chair and lead me out the door. I climbed into the car, but I remained silent until my father pulled into our driveway. He cut the engine and turned to me.

I lifted my gaze from the dashboard. "Why are they doing this to me?"

My father ran his fingers through his graying hair, making it stick on end. "To protect you."

"This is why you were crying earlier, isn't it? You knew they were sending me away," I stated.

He nodded solemnly.

"I don't get it, Dad. How could they even pull this off? I'm supposed to start school in a week."

He stared out the front of the car at the unopened garage door. "Carson has friends in high places. He can do almost anything he wants."

"I don't understand how this protects me," I protested.

"If that merman gets loose, he'll come after you—after anyone we've told of his existence," Dad said.

My voice shook. "That means we can't tell Mom. But you know about Tristan, which puts you in danger—yet you're sending *me* away."

Dad's hands tightened on the steering wheel. "I'm

prepared to stay and assist the council in these matters. I don't wish for you to be a part of this."

"So that's it?" I demanded. "I'm leaving? Will I ever be able to come back?"

Dad's eyes glistened, and his voice cracked. "I hope so."

Something told me I shouldn't hold my breath.

CHAPTER 4

The sound of an engine came from behind us, and I went still as my mother's car pulled into the driveway next to ours.

"Does she know?" I asked my dad.

"She doesn't know everything, but she knows you're leaving."

I cleared my throat. "And I can't tell her the truth?"

"It will be better that way."

As long as she didn't know about Tristan, Carson couldn't send her away like he was doing to me. She'd be able to stay here by the ocean, where she belonged.

I hated that man more than ever.

I still wasn't entirely convinced I'd be headed on a plane to a new school in a few hours. I was betting on the alternative —they were going to drop me out of the plane without a parachute. Carson Ray would probably do the honors himself. I did my best to hide these thoughts as I clicked the door open and stepped out onto the concrete to greet my mother.

She'd already exited her vehicle and stood with outstretched arms. "Bree, honey! I heard about your recommendation from Mrs. Ray. Congratulations!"

My whole body froze for a beat. She was *happy* about this? I forced my feet to continue moving, and I fell into her arms. Her frame was so much smaller than my father's, and her blue nurse scrubs were itchy against my bare arms. I wasn't sure how she managed to wear them all day at the clinic. Her brown hair—the same shade as mine—danced slightly in the breeze and tickled my nose.

I pulled away from her and forced a smile. "Yeah, I guess I have a real knack for journalism."

"I'm just sad you're leaving," Mom said.

I shrugged. "I was going to head to college in a week anyway."

"I know, but you would've still been in Sea Haven. You would've been able to visit every day. Now you'll be halfway across the country." Her smile quickly turned to a frown.

"It's great news, really," my father said, taking a step toward us. "It's not like she's the first young adult in Sea Haven to leave for college."

"Right," my mom agreed before looking back at me. "If you want a career in journalism, then you have to follow your dreams. It's great news that you got in—although, they're kind of late on sending out their acceptance letters, huh?"

"I was on a waiting list," I lied.

"I'm so proud of you, Bree," she raved.

Proud of me for uncovering secrets and being sent away so I don't spill them? I thought, but I simply smiled back instead.

"Not many teens are willing to leave Sea Haven after high school. You're going to come back with so much insight about the world. You're going to learn so much!" Mom said.

I quickly looked to my father to gauge his reaction. He kept his eyes locked on my mother, and I couldn't read him. I knew he was avoiding my gaze.

I turned back to my mother. "I really don't want to say goodbye."

Her expression softened. "I know. But remember, it's only four years, and you'll be back over holiday breaks and summer vacation. And hey, we can have a going away party for you."

My heart broke. She seemed awfully excited to see me leave Sea Haven.

"Uh, Carol," my father stepped in.

She turned to him, curious eyebrows raised.

"Bree has to leave for school tonight."

"What?" She looked between me and my father. "No, not tonight."

My father and I nodded solemnly in unison.

"No." Her voice cracked. "I'm not ready to say goodbye yet. This is... all so sudden." She placed her hand to her head like she was afraid she might pass out.

I couldn't bear to see her like this. "It's okay, Mom. We'll throw a going away party of our own. What do you say to whipping up some of your famous chocolate chip cookies?"

Her eyes lit up. "But, Bree, you never want to cook with me."

This may be my last chance. I smiled back at her. "Well, I'm going to need some cookies for the road."

My mom offered to wash my laundry while I said goodbye to my friends. When Liana didn't answer my text asking to meet up, I stepped out the back door and headed toward the beach. I hoped she would be there. If I didn't catch her before I had to leave, I'd never forgive myself for not saying goodbye.

At the beach, I scanned the throng of people. By now, the crowd was even thicker than when we'd gone swimming earlier. I stood on my toes, hoping to find her lying on the sand or splashing in the waves. I didn't see her, but after a quick scan of the beach, I recognized her pink beach bag lying in the sand. A girl in a purple bikini bent down near Liana's bag.

"Christina!" I called, hurrying toward her.

My friend flipped her wet braids out of her face and scanned the crowd.

"Christina!" I called again, closer this time.

Finally, she spotted me. She straightened up and took a swig from her water bottle.

"Hey, girl," she greeted after she swallowed. "What are you *wearing*? You're at the beach in jeans?"

"I stopped by looking for you and Liana. Do you two want to come over?"

She smiled, revealing a dimple on her left cheek. "Sure. We were almost done anyway." Christina pointed her chin toward the water as she rummaged through her bag. "Here Liana comes now."

"Hey!" Liana bent to her bag and pulled out a towel. "What's up?"

Christina spoke while drying off. "Bree asked if we wanted to hang at her place for a while."

"Sure, sounds fun," Liana agreed.

On the walk back to my house, dread overcame me. I had no idea how I was going to explain this all to them.

Back at my house, we headed straight to my bedroom. *Well, that's one way to tell them*, I thought when I opened my door. On my bed sat a huge suitcase we hadn't used in years. The last time I remembered seeing it was when my dad went on a business trip a few years go. My mom must've pulled it out of her closet for me. It was still covered in a thin layer of dust.

"Going somewhere?" Christina asked, plopping her beach bag onto my bed next to the suitcase. She pulled her coverall out of it and slipped it on. Liana did the same from near the doorway.

I bit my lip and turned to them. "Actually, yeah. I am."

"Packing for college already?" Liana wondered.

I took a deep breath and sat on my bed across from Christina. Liana sank to the floor by my closet and crossed her legs.

"Yes, actually... but not the college you think." I did my best to avoid their gazes and instead poked at a stray thread coming out of my jeans.

"What are you talking about?" Christina shifted from the opposite side of the bed.

I sighed. There was no easy way to say it. "I'm leaving Sea Haven."

"You're *what?*" Liana shot up from the floor.

Christina's jaw dropped, like she couldn't believe it. Honestly, neither could I.

"I got into a good college in Illinois. I'm leaving tonight," I told them.

"You're kidding, right?" Liana asked.

"I'm serious. I got in last minute, and I have to go. It's a really good opportunity for me." My gut twisted at the lie.

Christina narrowed her eyes like she didn't believe me. "You can't move across the country."

"Yeah," Liana agreed. "We're supposed to be room-mates! Why didn't you say anything about this before?"

I didn't want to leave her, and here she was *blaming* me like it was my decision.

"I thought you were undecided anyway," Liana added. "Why can't you at least get your gen eds out of the way here?"

"It's a good school," I told them. I actually had no idea. I didn't even know the name of the school I was being shipped off to; I didn't catch that during our meeting earlier. All I could focus on at the time was that it was halfway across the country where I'd be far, *far* away from the ocean.

"A good school for what?" Liana placed a hand on her hip. "Is it a party school? I know you said you weren't sure what you wanted to major in and you just wanted to go have a good time, but you can do that here!"

"Yeah, what's wrong with our university?" Christina asked.

I hated this. "I'm going to be a journalist." I forced myself not to say, *I guess*. It wasn't exactly my choice.

"Since when did you want to be a journalist?" Liana asked.

I shrugged, but inside of me, a fire burned. It took all I had to hold that fire in. "I don't know. It's just something I'm going to do." I couldn't even manage to spit out the lie and tell them I wanted to do it, but neither of them seemed to notice that it wasn't my choice. Still, they chewed me out like it was, like I was somehow betraying them.

"This isn't another one of your spontaneous decisions, is it?" Liana demanded. "I know you're always saying you'll figure things out as you go, but this is a big deal!"

"People don't just *leave* Sea Haven," Christina added.

"Yeah, they do," I said like it happened all the time, but it didn't. Only one or two people left per year, and I was beginning to wonder if the council had anything to do with sending them away. It's not like there was a *reason* to leave. Sea Haven was a happy place—the *happiest*.

"And you're leaving *tonight*?" Christina confirmed in disbelief.

I nodded. "But you know what? Now you two can be roommates."

Christina's shoulders fell. "We're really going to miss you."

"I know." My voice broke, and then suddenly, my friends were by my side, curling me into an embrace.

It was like watching my own funeral.

CHAPTER 5

After helping me pack my suitcase, my friends said their final goodbyes. My heart broke as I led them out the front door and watched them disappear down the sidewalk.

I'd managed to fit as many keepsakes as I could in the suitcase. I made sure to pack photographs, including my baby book, several framed photos of me with my family and friends, and most of the pictures that hung from the bulletin board above my bed. I packed the collection of illustrated mermaid stories my grandmother had given me as a kid before she died. I even made sure to pack the dolphin t-shirt Liana had given me last Christmas, even though I never wore it. From Christina, I packed the striped shell she'd found on the beach.

There was just one more thing I couldn't leave home without. I pulled the necklace from my jewelry box and held it up in front of my face. On the chain hung a small vial with a cork on top. The vial was filled with a small amount of sand and a blue-green liquid. My dad had picked it up from a tourist trap years ago on one of his trips down the coast.

I tugged at the cork. The darn thing didn't budge. I tried again, but I quickly noticed that by twisting it, I was beginning to rip the cork apart. I threw open a drawer at my desk and pulled out the safety pin I knew would be there. I shoved the pin between the cork and the edge of the glass, working my way around it to separate the glue. Finally, the cork broke free.

I hurried to the bathroom and poured the liquid down the drain. I didn't care about tossing the sand down, too, since there wasn't much of it. I quickly rinsed the vial to remove any last grains of sand, until it was completely empty.

Stepping out onto the back patio, I inhaled the scent of ocean air. It may be my last chance to enjoy the aroma of home. As a wave of tranquility washed over me, I took a step and then another and another until my feet hit wet sand. I bent and scooped a small amount of it into my vial. Nearby, a tiny shell caught my eye, and I threw that into the vial, too. Standing, I took another deep breath and walked until the ocean waves began lapping at my bare feet. As the next wave came in, I guided the water upward with my magic. I gathered just enough salt water droplets in my vial to fill it the rest of the way.

My racing heart settled as I held up the vial. Carson Ray may be able to take me out of Sea Haven, but he could *never* take Sea Haven away from me.

I returned to my bedroom, where I placed a dab of glue back on the cork and pressed it into the top of the vial. Then I slung the chain around my neck and tucked it under my shirt for safe keeping. I eyed the mirror to make sure it wasn't visible. It wasn't, but when I caught a glimpse of my face, a frown formed across it.

I hated that I was going along with this.

I turned from the mirror and fell down onto my bed next to the suitcase, burying my face into my pillow.

"Bree," my mom called from outside my room, making me jump.

I sat up straight in bed just as the door popped open a crack.

"How's it going? Almost all packed?" She poked her head into the room.

I nodded, but I couldn't keep that frown from returning to my face. "Almost."

She stepped through the doorway and sat on the bed. I glanced at the suitcase next to me. I wanted to hide her in there and take her along with me.

The plastic bag she held in her lap crinkled as she opened it.

"What's that?" I asked.

She sighed. "I picked up a few things for you. I knew you couldn't take too many liquids on the plane, so I bought you some travel sized shampoo and conditioner to hold you over until you can pick up more."

She pulled them from the bag and set them on top of the suitcase. "I thought you might like some other things for your dorm room, too. Here are some tacks for your bulletin board."

She set those aside as well but kept her eyes locked inside the bag, avoiding my gaze. "I also picked up some hand towels and a mini sewing kit, just some things I thought you might need. You have enough notebooks and pencils, right? Because I didn't get you any."

"Mom," I stopped her just as her bottom lip began to quiver. "It's okay."

She didn't let my words slow her down. "And, you know, I figured you'll need to buy some stuff once you're there, so... here." She reached into her back pocket and shoved an envelope in my direction.

I furrowed my brow. "What's this?"

She gestured for me to take it.

I did, and when I flipped the top open, I couldn't believe how much cash was in there. "Mom, I don't need this... really."

"Yes, you do." She spoke softly, her eyes now brimming with tears.

"I don't. I'll get a job or something while I'm out there."

"It's just to start you off," she insisted. "You're going to need to buy a clothes hamper, a trash can, textbooks... There's just so much to get, and I... I can't be there with you." Her voice cracked, and my heart shattered.

"Mom." I leaned over and wrapped her in a hug. "It's going to be okay. I promise. I'll still call you. We can video chat. It will be just like if I went to college in Sea Haven."

Was that even true?

I wasn't going to pretend to even *try* making sense of this madness. From the moment I discovered Tristan on the beach, nothing made sense anymore. The best I could do was play along with the council's game and hope no one else got sent away because of me. Being exiled from your own home was literally *the worst*.

But I didn't have a choice.

"Yeah, but you won't be here," my mother said.

"I have a few more hours." It was all I could offer. "Are you ready to make cookies?"

Her expression softened, and she smiled. "Absolutely."

I swallowed down the lump in my throat as I hoisted my suitcase off my bed. This all felt like a dream.

This can't be happening. Wake up, Bree. Wake up!

It didn't matter how many times I wished myself out of the situation. My magic didn't work that way.

"Are you ready?" my father asked, peeking his head through my open door.

I glanced around the room one last time. Photographs

of my friends and me at the tide pools hung off my bulletin board, and jars of sand art lined my dresser. I made a jar every summer and filled it with shells and other treasures Liana, Christina, and I had found at the beach. The trophy I'd won during the Sea Festival swim competition my freshman year of high school sat on my shelf next to the books Dad had given me. I'd wanted to read his favorite book series, but I hadn't gotten around to it yet. The dresses I'd bought the last time Mom and I went shopping still hung in the closet, and the caricature the three of us had gotten when I was a kid was framed above my dresser. I couldn't believe I was leaving all this behind.

I turned back to my father. "I guess I'm ready."

Mom stepped past him and pulled me into a hug. "Are you sure you got enough cookies?"

She'd placed the whole batch in a container for me, and I'd packed it in my luggage. I wasn't sure it'd last me to the airport. I wouldn't be able to savor her homemade cookies forever.

"I have enough, Mom," I told her.

"Okay." She squeezed me one last time. "I hope you have a lot of fun in college. Be sure to stay in touch."

I shot her a reassuring smile. "I will."

I didn't know what would happen once I left, or if the council would somehow prevent me from contacting my family and friends. For good measure, I'd buried my phone and charger in the deepest depths of my suitcase and then slipped my old phone in my pocket as a dummy. It's not like taking away my phone would stop me, though. I'd have access to computers at the college's library.

If I make it that far, I thought.

"Here, let me get that," my father said, reaching for my suitcase.

"Bye, Mom. I love you."

"Bye, sweetie!"

She stood at the front door and waved goodbye as I followed behind my father toward his car. He loaded the bag into his trunk before crossing to the driver's side door. I reluctantly slid into the passenger seat.

"Dad?" I asked once he pulled out of the driveway.

"Yeah?" His gaze flickered over to me, but his hands tightened on the steering wheel.

My voice came out soft, so soft I wasn't sure he heard me. "Am I going to be all right?"

His face fell, and he reached over to grab my hand. A tight squeeze meant to reassure me didn't help as much as I would have liked it to. "Of course you're going to be okay."

I swallowed hard, and my voice came out louder this time. "Then why are you so afraid?"

"Because I'm going to miss you. We're going to figure this out, and then you'll be able to come home."

I crossed my arms and leaned back in my chair. "You can't promise that. How can you be sure Carson Ray isn't going to drop me out of the plane?"

My father seemed taken aback, like it was ludicrous to ever suggest such a thing. "Nobody's going to *drop you out of a plane*. I mean it. You're going to be okay."

"Yeah, okay," I said just as he parked in front of City Hall. I made sure he couldn't miss the sarcasm in my voice. I stepped out of the car and slammed the car door behind me.

Why did it feel like my father was walking me to my own execution?

CHAPTER 6

My father told me to leave my suitcase in the back until the car taking me to the airport showed up. Until then, he said we had to meet with *Mr. Ray*.

"Miss Waters." Carson smiled as my father and I entered his office.

I didn't return the gesture.

An older man with white hair and wrinkles around his eyes stood next to Carson. I recognized him from the clinic, though he'd never been my doctor. He wore a blue button-down shirt, and his hands were stuffed into the pockets of his tan pants.

"I trust you're familiar with Dr. Sloan," Carson said, gesturing to the man. "We might as well get started right away. Follow me, please."

I wondered briefly what we needed a doctor for. I glared at him as Carson passed by us to lead the way.

Dad stepped in front of him. "Please, Carson. This can't be necessary. She's only eighteen."

"I'm afraid it's a requirement," Carson said as he stepped past him. "We can't risk it, even for your daughter."

"You told me she wouldn't have to go through with this," my dad growled.

"I told you she would be safe," Carson countered.

I had no idea what they were talking about. Carson was out the door before I could ask.

I followed him down the hall with my father at my side. My dad didn't look too happy.

I held my head high. "I have some questions."

Carson stopped in front of the elevator and pressed a button. "I can't promise you'll get the answer you want."

The four of us stepped into the elevator.

"Will I ever be able to come back?" I held my breath, fearing the answer.

Carson kept his gaze locked ahead as the elevator descended. "We hope you will."

Silence hung in the air, and it made me really uncomfortable. The elevator doors opened to reveal a hallway with a concrete floor and cinderblock walls. Several doors with small windows and a different number on each lined the hall. The air was cold, and the basement was eerily dim.

Carson stepped out first. "I don't expect you to understand, Miss Waters, and for that, I am truly sorry."

I didn't believe him.

Sending me away didn't ensure my silence. They might as well cut out my tongue and cut off my fingers if they didn't want me to say anything. But, as I walked down the dark basement hallway and nervously glanced at each passing door, a shiver ran down my spine. I knew fear was enough to shut me up, and I had no doubt they knew that, too. I didn't want to put my friends and family in danger.

I followed behind Carson as he turned to the right where the hall came to a T. I glanced into each of the small windows on the doors as we passed, hoping for some indication of where they were taking me. This wasn't exactly the place for a limo service. The rooms were all black inside.

"Where are we going?" I asked boldly. Immediately, my heart rate spiked, and my hands shook at my sides. I wanted to be brave, but I wasn't even fooling myself.

Nobody answered.

We passed by a door with its light on. The others seemed to rush by it, but my gaze locked on the window. I saw nothing but bare walls. Then, just for a moment, I swear a shadow crossed my line of sight. My father placed his hand on my back, startling me.

Carson stopped in front of a door further down the hall, and Dr. Sloan stepped forward and placed a silver key into it. The end was hooked like an ocean wave, reminding me of the logo on the front of the building. I wondered if it was a master key.

"Right here, Miss Waters," Carson said. "We'll explain as much as we can in a moment."

I didn't know what I expected to find, but when I stepped into the room, it didn't look promising. The floor was carpeted, but with no windows, poor lighting, and the same cinderblock walls as in the hall, it wasn't exactly inviting.

The room was small, and there was another door to our right with a keypad mounted beside it. The only piece of furniture was a red chair with metal legs placed at the center of the room. All it was missing was the spotlight, and I'd say you had yourself an interrogation room.

"Please, take a seat, Miss Waters." Carson gestured to the chair.

Oh, God. This is *an interrogation room. Are they going to torture me? I'd tell them anything if they just asked!*

I shot my father a worried expression. He nodded to tell me it'd be okay. My knees shook, and I sat in the chair as I was told. The plastic was cold against my legs.

Carson approached me. "Please understand, Miss Waters, this is merely a precaution. I've asked your father to be here to oversee the procedure."

The procedure? Were they going to do surgery on me or something?

He continued. "This isn't going to hurt a bit."

What were they going to do to me? I gripped the seat

of my chair so tightly that the plastic began to dig into the skin on my fingers.

"Carson, you're terrifying her!" my father snapped.

"Please just tell me what's going on," I begged. Was it their prime goal to scare me to death? Was that how they were going to dispose of me?

"There's a reason our kind sticks together," Carson said coldly. "No one may leave Sea Haven with their magic."

I couldn't have heard him right. I spoke slowly, my tone wavering. "But I *do* have magic. Does that mean... I'm not leaving?"

Carson laughed, and it chilled my bones. "Your magic will be extracted."

My grip tightened on the chair. "You can't do that!"

"They can," Dad admitted solemnly. "It's Sea Haven law. Every business trip I've been on has required it."

A lump rose to my throat, but I swallowed it down. "How's that even possible?"

"Dr. Sloan will harness your magic," Carson said. "I assure you that he's very good at what he does. There's nothing to worry about."

Nothing to worry about? Let's see you sit in this chair, and we'll harness your magic.

Dr. Sloan stepped forward. "It's a simple magical procedure in which I will extract your core, and you will be free to leave. Should you ever return to Sea Haven, you may restore your core."

He couldn't be serious. Our core was like our spirit and was very sacred to our people. It was the origin of our magic and what allowed us to harness the powers of the sea. I'd never seen one, but I knew my core as deeply as I knew my soul.

"No! Please," I cried. "I want to keep my magic."

"I'm afraid that's not possible," Carson said coldly. "It is necessary to protect you. If anyone on the outside world learns what you can do, they will capture you, and then come after us all. Your core must remain in Sea Haven."

My whole body trembled. "I won't say anything. I swear. Just please don't take my magic!"

Carson frowned. "There's no need to turn this into an ordeal. Dr. Sloan, please continue."

The doctor reached out for me, but I dodged his hand and slipped under his arm. I leapt from my chair and lunged toward the door. My fingers barely grazed the metal knob before an arm wrapped around my waist, pulling me back.

"Get off me!" I kicked and flailed my arms with all my strength, but it was to no avail.

The arms around me tightened, pulling me back to the red plastic chair. Why had I let them bring me down here? Why didn't I just run away while I had the chance? I could have slipped out of Sea Haven and hitchhiked my way far across the country where they couldn't torture me. I didn't know where I would have started. I'd never been out of Sea Haven before, but I was sure I could figure something out.

"Stop! No!" I cried again, swinging an elbow at my assailant's face. It connected with a thud just before he dropped me into the chair. I looked up to see who I'd hit.

Surprise slammed into me when I found my father's face staring down at me.

My father. The man who used to read me a story every night before I fell asleep. The man who'd taught me how to swim and ride a bike. The man who'd watched horror movies with me when I didn't want to watch them alone.

The man I would have once trusted with my life.

"Dad…?" I could hardly get the word out as I stared up at him.

His gaze fell. "Bree, please do as they say."

It was clear all Dad wanted was to protect me, and he was terrified.

Before I could make another attempt at an escape, at fighting the three men off, Dr. Sloan's hand rested on my head. I caught a glimpse of something in his hand—a rock of some sort—before his fingers curled around it and his hand began to glow.

That's when the agony hit. My chest tightened, and my stomach hollowed all at the same time, as if someone had reached into my abdomen and ripped all my insides out at once.

"Please," I begged one last time. My voice came out as barely a whisper as all my energy drained from my body.

CHAPTER 7

Council head Carson Ray was a liar. He said it wouldn't hurt, but it did. It may not have hurt in a physical sense, but it was emotionally excruciating. I could *feel* my magic drain out of me as if it was my blood itself. In some ways, it felt as if the whole building had collapsed on me. No. Not the building. My whole world. Everything I knew had fallen apart.

Dr. Sloan released me. I tried to blink the world into focus, but my head swam. When the dizziness settled, I noticed a small glass vial in Dr. Sloan's hand. It clinked against the stone he held. The vial glowed a bright blue, and I couldn't tear my eyes off it. I straightened in the chair and leaned forward, wanting nothing more than to touch it, than to hold it, than for it to be mine.

I blinked several more times, and that's when I realized it *was* mine. Dr. Sloan held my magic in physical form—my core. It was so beautiful, so mesmerizing. The glow danced and shifted as if my magic was fluid, alive. It was entrancing.

Dr. Sloan turned from me, blocking my view of the vial that held my magic. Anguish tangled in my gut.

"You can't do this to me!" I attempted to stand from my chair, but without my magic running through my veins, I couldn't find my balance.

Dr. Sloan slid a golden key into the door beside us and entered a code on the keypad. He tried to shield my view, but I saw the numbers he entered—2673. The keypad beeped, then he turned the key, and the door opened.

Carson and my father stepped toward me, but I couldn't bear to look at them. All I could do was stare after Dr. Sloan, longing for him to bring my magic back to me.

"Miss Waters." Carson's voice somehow cut through the sound of my own pulse beating against the sides of my skull. "I understand how hard this must be for you."

He understood nothing.

"Bree," my father said softly, placing a hand on my shoulder.

I shook him off. "Don't, Dad," I snapped. "You just stood there! How could you do this to me?"

He stepped back.

"Let's just give her a minute," Carson told my father.

If they said anything else, I didn't hear it. The room seemed to shrink around me, and the sound of voices faded. Even though they stood right next to me, I felt utterly alone.

Empty.

I didn't want to be in this room anymore. If they wanted me to feel alone, then so be it. I wanted nothing more than to get far, *far* away from any of them.

Anger surged through me, and I shot out of my chair. It took all I had not to topple back over.

"Let's just get this over with," I insisted through gritted teeth. I only hoped they were being honest when they said they were sending me to Illinois, that I wouldn't get on a plane and end up at the bottom of the ocean. It's not like my magic could help me there anymore.

Carson forced a cold smile. "Right this way, Miss Waters."

Dr. Sloan emerged back out of the door he'd just entered. I caught only a glimpse of the far wall, just enough to see that the room was as big as the one we were standing in. He slid the golden key into the lock and clicked it shut, then placed the key back into his pocket and followed the rest of us out into the hall.

We were halfway down the hall when movement caught my eye. I paused and stared into the room with its light on. That shadow I'd noticed before crossed the small window once again. What was it about this room that its light was on when all of the others remained pitch black?

"This way, Miss Waters," Carson snapped.

I glanced at him, but I couldn't help but steal one more look into the room's window. In that moment, shock hit me straight in the gut. Starting at me through the sliver of glass was a pair of blue-green eyes.

"Tristan," I whispered so softly that I barely heard myself. I couldn't move even though I knew I was obligated to follow the three men.

"Follow me," Carson sneered, though his voice sounded far off, like my head was under water. A hand gripped around my bicep and pulled me from the door. "We're on a schedule, and you don't want to miss your flight."

My feet moved under me, though I hadn't consciously decided to move. Carson managed to pull me far enough away that I could no longer see Tristan's eyes. I straightened as he released me, and I finally found my feet, but the shock hadn't yet faded. They were keeping Tristan prisoner down here—a man so powerful he could destroy our entire town. A shiver traveled down my spine.

My father and Dr. Sloan turned down the hall toward the elevators, and that's when Carson stopped me.

He stood in front of me, blocking my path, and leaned so close I could feel his breath on my face. "That man is very dangerous. I'm sure you understand that speaking of this could result in *consequences.*"

My knees shook. They'd just stolen my magic from me because I saw something I shouldn't have. They should be *thanking* me that I found Tristan before the rest of the town woke and spotted him lying on the beach. Instead, they were sending me away. I didn't want to know what else they'd take from me if I spoke of this to anyone.

I swallowed hard. "I understand."

"Good," he said, turning on his heel. "This way."

We turned down the hall we'd come from and made it to the elevators just as the doors opened. Nobody spoke as the elevator ascended to the first floor. Once we stepped out, Dr. Sloan nodded a goodbye and went on his way down the hall. I stared after him, my breathing shallow. How could he just walk away like that as if he didn't just do something horrible? Didn't they understand that what they'd just done to me was torture?

I barely processed my surroundings as I followed Carson back to his office. The ocean paintings and shell macrame that adorned these walls didn't register. The whole building felt empty.

I didn't want to follow him. I wanted to run, to get away, but what good would that do me? They already took the one thing most precious to me, the one thing I never thought I'd be without. Nothing mattered anymore. Nothing.

When we entered his office, Carson crossed the room to his desk and picked up a blue folder. He held it out to me, and I eyed it skeptically before taking it. I opened the folder and scanned the first page as he spoke.

"This is your travel itinerary along with your class schedule and any other information you'll need to get settled in. Due to your situation, the school has agreed to house you early in their dorms. Once your flight lands, a woman named Sharon Mitchel will be waiting for you at baggage claim. She'll drive you to the university and help you get settled in."

I briefly wondered what *situation* they'd told the school to get them to agree to this. The thought made my head swim, and the rest of Carson's explanations faded into the background.

"Can I go now?" I snapped, harsher than I intended. I couldn't stand to wait here in his office that looked like a courtroom any longer. It was like every look he gave me was in judgement and every word he said was a smack of the gavel followed by my prison sentence. At this point, it felt like I was in for life. Without my magic, I'd be living in my own personal hell. And I didn't want to spend it here.

Carson glanced at his watch. "Your car should be here. This way."

As we exited the building, the warm summer night air hit me. I noticed the black sedan right away. It didn't quite have the same look as Carson's car I'd seen him in the other night, but it was similarly ominous.

"I'll grab your suitcase," my father offered.

I didn't even bother with a smile.

Carson went to talk to the driver, and my father returned quickly with my bag. He slapped the backend of the car, and the driver responded by popping the trunk. My father hauled my suitcase into it before turning to me.

"Bree," he said softly. "I know this isn't easy. Once this has been sorted out, you'll be able to return. Stay safe. I love you."

He reached out for me, but I pulled away. My heart broke to do it. I mean, he was my dad. I *did* love him. But he'd failed to protect me. He let them steal a part of me. No. He didn't just *let* them. He *helped* them.

"I'd like to go now," I whispered in a broken tone.

My father's face fell, but he opened the back door for me. I slid into the black leather seat behind the driver, and my dad placed my backpack on the seat next to me. All I could do was stare forward as the torment of loss clenched in my stomach.

Carson caught the door before my father could close it. He leaned into the car and whispered so softly that even the driver couldn't hear. "You will speak of this to no human soul. I know people like you. You never leave well enough alone, but you will get on that plane, Miss Waters, and you will finish this."

A chill traveled down my spine, and I knew I had no choice but to follow his orders. Carson slammed the door, and the driver pulled away from City Hall.

I thought that being exiled was the worst thing they could do to me. I was wrong. I could live without Sea Haven. I could even survive without the ocean. But I couldn't do it without my magic. No one should have the right—the power—to take that away from me.

The driver never spoke, and I liked it that way. I gripped on to the necklace I'd slipped on earlier and stared ahead as an all-consuming emptiness filled my chest.

I didn't know how much time had passed, but eventually, we made it to the city.

I straightened up from where I'd been slumped against the car's window. My joints and muscles ached for remaining in such an uncomfortable position for so long. I didn't say anything, and neither did my driver. It was strange. I had no idea who was sitting in the front seat, no idea if I could trust him. He had broad shoulders and dark, buzzed hair, but that was all I could see of him. What was his story? Did he have to give up his magic, too? Or was it just me?

"You okay back there?" the driver asked. He had a deep, masculine voice, but I didn't recognize it, not that I expected to. I may have been familiar with almost every face in Sea Haven, but that didn't mean I knew everyone personally.

I cleared my throat. "Are we almost there?"

"Just a few more minutes," he assured me.

It wasn't long before we pulled up to the airport. He stopped the car and popped the trunk.

"You have everything you need?" he asked.

I grabbed my backpack and the blue folder from the back seat. "I do. Just need to grab my bag."

For the first time, the man glanced back at me. I recognized his blue eyes and strong jawline. His name was Jarod Erickson, and he worked with my father. I never knew he was their errand boy, though. Unless that's not what he was. He could be a hit man.

I quickly scrambled out of the car at the thought and hurried to the trunk, where I heaved my bag onto the pavement. Hastily, I slammed the car's trunk and headed for the building. Only once I was inside did I take a breath. If he really was going to kill me, he would have driven me to some deserted field and shot me there.

I opened my folder to get the information I needed about my flight. I checked in and made it through security. The whole time, the hair on the back of my neck stood. I remained focused on the task at hand, reminding myself that this was almost over, and soon I'd be far away from Sea Haven and could put all this behind me.

It was a lie, though. I wasn't going to be able to put any of this behind me. *Ever*.

But I couldn't ditch my plane ride. With the way things were going, they had to be monitoring my every move. They'd know if I didn't get on the plane.

Calm down, I told myself. *They aren't following you.*

I didn't want to take the chance that I was right.

CHAPTER 8

The water never looked so peaceful as it did today.

"Come on, Daddy. What are you waiting for?" I turned my gaze from the horizon and back toward my father. My voice sounded higher pitched than it should.

My father and I were the only two on the beach, and it was the perfect day for a swim. For some reason, he'd forgotten his swim trunks. He stood on the sandy beach in a black suit, his hands shoved in his pockets.

"You go ahead without me," he offered with a smile.

I returned a happy grin. "Are you going to time how long I can stay under the water?"

"Sure." He adjusted the watch on his wrist. "Last time you stayed under for an hour and a half. Think you can do better this time?"

I gazed down at my feet in shame. My toenails seemed so small and were painted a bright red. They matched the polka dotted one-piece I was wearing.

"Yeah, Daddy," I told him. "I just got bored last time."

"But you're from Sea Haven," he pointed out. "You know that people from Sea Haven can stay under water for hours."

"Not if they get hungry, Daddy," I pointed out.

When he laughed, his eyes crinkled at the corners. "You're right."

I squinted toward him to keep the sun from my eyes. Brown bangs tickled my eyelashes. I didn't remember cutting my hair. The last time I'd had bangs was when I was seven.

"I can stay under water longer. I won't get bored or hungry or anything," I promised.

He pressed his lips together. "I don't know. I'm not sure you can do it."

"Of course I can, Daddy. Watch me!"

I splashed into the water until my head dipped beneath the surface. I inhaled a breath of water, but the moment I did, pain hit me. My nostrils burned, and my lungs felt as if they were failing. Pressure built up inside my body. I tried again, but that only accented the pain. Pressure against the top of my skull made me panic. I pressed my feet against the sand to push myself toward *the surface, but despite my best efforts, I remained in place.*

What was going on?

I turned my gaze toward the surface of the water, hoping to discover an answer. What I found was more horrifying than I could have ever imagined.

Dark storm clouds had rolled in. Against the dark of the sky, I could make out a shadow. Carson Ray stared down at me, his features distorted from the rippling water. An evil grin spread across his face as he held my head under water so I couldn't breathe.

I woke with a start and inhaled a deep breath. The woman next to me on the plane shot me an odd stare. I quickly relaxed and rested my head back against my headrest while I stared out the window.

It was only a dream, I repeated to myself. I forced myself to take three deep breaths, but it didn't help.

I remained silent the rest of the plane ride. As I waited for passengers near the front to exit the plane first, I pulled my blue folder out of my backpack and looked it over again. My itinerary told me I was to meet a woman named Sharon Mitchel at baggage claim. I sighed heavily and slipped the folder back into my bag before standing and slinging it across my shoulder.

After navigating through halls and following the signs to baggage claim, I arrived. I glanced around, but I didn't know who this woman was. Nobody in particular caught my eye, but I did notice a few people from my flight standing around one of the carousels. I joined them and waited for my bag. Just as I grabbed it and turned to find a place to wait, a woman's voice caught my attention.

"Bree Waters?"

I glanced up to find a tall woman smiling at me. She looked about my mother's age and wore a black pantsuit with heels. The smile on her face appeared genuine and friendly. I brushed my brown hair out of my eyes and returned the smile. Even she could probably tell it was fake.

"Yes," I told her.

"Hi," she greeted, sticking her hand in my direction. "I'm Sharon Mitchel."

I noticed her nails had been done recently. Mine, on the other hand, still had bits of sand under them.

"It's nice to meet you," I said, though my tone came out sounded stilted. We fell into step side by side.

"How was your flight?" she asked.

I shrugged, keeping my eyes on the signs around us. "It was okay. I slept through most of it."

"Are you excited to get started with classes?"

I resisted the shrug this time. At the mention of college classes, my mind wandered to a recurring daydream I'd had of Liana and me setting up our dorm room. Sadness washed over me at the thought that I'd never get to experience that with her. Would I even ever see her again? I quickly reminded myself of my phone in the bottom of my suitcase. No one had bothered to take the dummy phone from me, so I figured I'd be safe with my working phone. Unless they were going to use it to spy on me… I might have to buy a new one.

I realized how long I'd remained silent, and I forced myself to answer, even if it wasn't entirely true. "I guess so."

Sharon glanced over at me several times before speaking again. It was like she needed something to fill the silence. "You look like your mother."

"You know my mom?" I asked.

She looked at me questioningly while we walked. "I thought you knew. I'm from Sea Haven. I moved away years ago, and now I work in the admissions office at the university."

She didn't have to say the rest. In that moment, I understood how Carson managed to pull so many strings this close to the first day of school. He'd used Sharon. Only, wouldn't she have had to manipulate the records or something? Wasn't that fraud?

I noticed I'd fallen behind a few steps, so I quickened my pace to catch up. Sharon led me through a pair of doors that took us into a long hall that crossed above the road and into the parking garage.

I didn't know how much I could trust her, but my curiosity burned. "Why'd you leave?"

She clicked a button on her key fob, and a dark blue car blinked its lights in response. She shrugged. "I always felt like Sea Haven was too small of a town for me."

At the car, she popped open the back hatch and gestured for me to place my suitcase inside. When she closed the back, she spoke again. "I guess I was just always eager to see more of the world."

I opened the passenger side door and slid in as she rounded to the driver's side.

"Don't you miss the ocean?" I asked once we'd settled in.

"I did at first, but the pull of the ocean fades after a while. Now I don't think I could leave all this greenery and beauty here." She glanced sideways at me as she slowly drove toward the exit. "I know it's hard at first."

She had no clue... or maybe she did?

"Did they let you keep your magic?" I asked. If she knew what this was like, she wouldn't be saying these things.

She slowed behind another car at the exit. "No, Bree. No one leaves Sea Haven with their magic. It's the price we must pay when we choose to leave."

My thoughts honed in on one word. *Choose.*

"You chose to leave?" I asked in shock. She wasn't forced to leave like me? Why would anyone want to leave Sea Haven?

"Yes. I told you—Sea Haven wasn't big enough for me."

"Do you know why I left?" I asked challengingly. How much did she know?

She looked at me again before fixing her eyes back on the road. "No, and I didn't ask. What I do know is that

Carson Ray has a lot of secrets. I've learned not to press him about them, but I believe that he acts in everyone's best interests. I would expect nothing less of the head of Sea Haven's city council."

She had the first part of that right. Carson Ray had *a lot* of secrets, too many if you asked me. But I didn't believe he was watching out for *everyone's* best interests.

He certainly wasn't watching out for mine.

CHAPTER 9

Sharon asked me if I wanted a tour of the campus, but I declined, saying I was too tired from traveling. It wasn't just lack of sleep that got to me. I still felt physically drained from having my magic stolen from me, and everything that had happened in the past two nights left me feeling overwhelmed. I still hadn't had enough time to process it all.

Sharon helped me get settled into the dorms. She introduced me to the resident advisor and gave me some instructions about my room and my classes, but with enough already going on in my head, I had a difficult time adding all that new information to the list. The resident advisor gave me some form I had to fill out about damage to the room and anything that needed to be replaced. As soon as I entered the room, the bed looked so inviting that I set the paper on the dresser and fell onto it. I didn't even bother doing anything with my suitcase.

"I'll leave my phone number right here," Sharon told me. I heard her feet shuffle near the dresser. "That way you can call me if you have any questions, okay?"

I had already closed my eyes, and her words barely registered. "Thank you."

"See you later, Bree," she said, and I heard the door click behind her.

Relief washed over me. I'd made it this far. I hadn't been shot in the middle of a secluded field or dropped out of the plane without a parachute. Though it was early in the day and I should have been doing something productive, exhaustion overtook almost immediately, and I drifted off.

My hair billowed around me in the wind as I walked up the steps to City Hall. My expression remained emotionless, strong, and each step I took marked one step closer to revenge. Footsteps from multiple pairs of feet echoed behind me. I wasn't sure who was marching with me, but I knew they were friends. I reached the top of the stairs and pushed through the front doors of the building with purpose.

A pair of dark eyes stared back at me. Carson Ray stood

alone with his arms crossed over his chest and his feet planted firmly shoulder-width apart. It was as if he was waiting for me and took this stance to show his own strength. It wasn't going to work. He didn't scare me. He couldn't hurt me when I had all my friends with me.

"You're not going to get away with this," I said firmly.

An evil laugh bubbled up from his throat. "And I suppose you're going to stop me?"

My lips twitched into a grin. "Yes," I answered simply.

"Really?" He raised an eyebrow. "You and what army?"

I turned to see my friends weren't there. I placed two fingers in my mouth and whistled. Bodies began to filter through the front doors.

Sharon Mitchel entered first. She wore the same dark pantsuit I'd met her in, and her heels clicked against the floor as she came to stand next to me. She held her head high and pursed her lips, never taking her eyes off Carson.

Other people filled the City Hall entrance. Another face caught my eye. Noah Starr. I'd never known him well, but he'd been the talk of the school my junior year when he announced he was leaving Sea Haven for college. His eyes met mine, and he winked in my direction.

I recognized another girl who'd been two grades above me. There was a family of four that once lived on our street but left Sea Haven years ago because their father got a job in another city. The two daughters still looked around ten, the same age I remembered them being when they left.

Once I'd taken in several of the faces, I realized what

they all had in common. They'd all left Sea Haven, which meant they'd all been stripped of their magic.

And then the last two people I expected to see stepped through the door.

"Liana. Christina. They didn't take your magic too, did they?" I asked in surprise.

Liana shook her head. "No. We're here because what they're doing to you is unfair." She fell into my arms in an embrace.

"We're here to support you, Bree." Christina took me into her own hug after Liana drew away.

I swallowed deeply, pulling in as much courage as I could muster. Under my breath, I whispered to them both, "Carson Ray has no idea who he's dealing with."

I whirled back toward him. I could sense my two best friends behind me, their breathing so familiar.

A look of amusement settled over Carson's face. "Well, I didn't think you'd actually come with an army, Miss Waters."

I hated when he called me that. "Bree," I stated. "My name is Bree. You stole something from me, and I'm not leaving until I get it back."

He smiled slyly. "You may die trying, Miss Waters, but you're never going to get your magic back. It's mine now."

He pulled a small vial from his pocket and held it up in front of me, taunting me. Its blue hue drew me in. I felt its energy calling to me the way it had when Dr. Sloan extracted it from me. I reached for the vial, but Carson *pulled it away, holding it above my head like a schoolyard bully.*

Carson's little stunt left his chest exposed, vulnerable. In one swift motion, I pulled my arm back and then sent my open palm straight toward his chest. Carson stumbled back, gasping for air. His hands came to clutch his chest, and the vial he'd been holding fell into my outstretched palm.

Nobody tried to help Carson. I couldn't read everyone else's minds, but somehow I knew. As a collective unit, it was what we all wanted—to see Carson Ray suffer for what he'd done to us.

I gasped as I suddenly woke. It took me a moment to process my surroundings and realize I was in the dorm room they'd assigned me. I couldn't bring myself to call it *my* dorm room yet. If I had my way, I wouldn't be staying here long.

As soon as I woke fully, I shuffled through my bag for my phone and connected it to the dorm's Wi-Fi. I hadn't been gone that long, but I already missed my friends and family. I found several messages from my friends saying they missed me already and they wished me luck. My mom had messaged me, teasing about whether or not I'd eaten all the cookies already. That reminder sent me reaching for them, and I gobbled up three before I could remind myself to slow down. I nibbled on several more as I scrolled through my phone. Nobody asked how I liked it here; though I guess I hadn't been gone long enough for that. To them, I'd only been gone a few hours. To me, it already felt like a lifetime.

I didn't want to leave the room, but I had to use the bathroom. Sighing, I rose and headed down the hall.

After exiting the stall, I stood at the sink to wash my hands. The water felt refreshing as it flowed over my hands, but something about it felt *wrong*. I couldn't connect to it like I used to, and that sent an ache to settle in my gut. I cupped my palms together and bent to splash the water over my face, but it didn't help.

I needed more than a stream of water. I needed a bath or a pool or something I could submerge myself in. I shut off the faucet, and an eerie silence settled over the room. After drying my hands, I returned to the dorm room they'd assigned me. There, I grabbed the stack of papers the resident advisor had given me and shuffled through them. I thought I'd seen a welcome pamphlet she said had a list of activities in it. She'd said there was a pool here, didn't she? But where?

I found the pamphlet and flipped through it until I found mention of the pool and its hours. My heart dropped when I discovered the rec center wasn't open until school started. I flipped through another few pages. A photograph of a lake caught my eye. It was so strange to see such a small body of water. I was used to water as far as the eye could see. This lake couldn't have been more than two acres, but at least it was something. I quickly read through the information and saw there was a small swimming area with no hour restrictions. I checked the campus map at the front of the pamphlet to figure out how to get there.

I hopped up from the bed and pulled on my swimming suit, then hurried across campus.

The swimming area was empty when I arrived. The lake was different than the ocean back home. The water had a brownish-green tint to it, and when I looked a few feet out, it was so murky I couldn't see the bottom. Small waves danced across the surface of the water, but the crashing waves I was so used to didn't exist here.

I stepped forward. The water hit my knees, sending excited jitters throughout my body. I loved the water. How could Sharon say she didn't miss it anymore?

The water rose to my chest. As soon as I walked out far enough that the water licked at the bottom of my chin, nerves overtook. What would happen when I went under water? Would I be able to breathe?

I swallowed my fear, pinched my nose shut, and dipped my head beneath the surface. A sense of comfort washed over me. The water felt so inviting, so much like home. I opened my eyes, and although the water was calmer and murkier than back home, the way the light filtered in and danced off the sand near shore was mesmerizing.

My lungs began to ache the longer I held my breath. I dropped my fingers from my nose but didn't draw in a breath. Still, I was curious. Without my magic, was I only human, or did I still have some of my merfolk ancestry running through my veins? I always thought of it as a constant, as something I'd always have, like my heartbeat or my thoughts.

It felt as if a weight was lying on my chest, and I couldn't take it anymore. Opening my airways, I sucked in a breath. Water filled my mouth and my nostrils. Normally, this action would provide relief. Today, it only brought pain.

An image flashed before my eyes. In my imagination, the water around me changed color to a clearer blue, and Carson Ray stood above me, holding my head under water. In an instant, the image I'd seen in my dream disappeared.

I quickly kicked off the sandy bottom of the pond and then inhaled a long, deep breath as cold air hit my face. I sputtered water, and suddenly, my pulse spiked. When I tried to find my footing, I couldn't reach the bottom. My arms flailed in an attempt to swim back toward shallower waters. I stretched my toes out as far as I could to feel for the bottom without letting my head go under again. I commanded the water to hold me up, until I remembered it wouldn't respond.

Finally, the ends of my toes brushed against something solid. I swam forward several more feet until I could stand. Inhaling another long breath, I let myself relax as I waded toward shore.

I fell to my hands and knees in the shallow water, then rolled onto my back in the sand, panting. I didn't completely exit the water. It enveloped me like an embrace, and it was the closest thing I had to remind me of the ocean. I closed my eyes and tried to picture myself at home, but I couldn't. Everything felt wrong. The water wasn't the right temperature, it lacked that salty smell, and the sun definitely wasn't as warm and friendly as I was used to.

I might as well have been lying at the deepest depths of the ocean, because that's what the crushing weight on my chest felt like. I didn't know who I was without my magic.

What does it matter anyway? I asked myself. I shifted onto my side and curled my knees to my chest. Tears beaded at the corners of my eyes. My magic had never been that powerful. All I could do was breathe under water and manipulate small amounts of water. It's not like I could control the weather or compel others with a siren call like our ancestors could.

So what's my magic good for anyway? I wondered. *I'm not a mermaid. I'm just some crossbred mutt whose magic is hardly magic at all.*

My heart sank, and I hated myself for thinking that way. My magic may have not been that fantastic, but it was *mine.* Without my core, the essence of who I was and who I was born to be ceased to exist. I felt powerless, empty, and alone.

Every piece of me felt like it was slowly fading away, until I couldn't feel the cold water on my skin any longer. I'd gone completely numb.

There was no worse feeling in the world.

All I wanted was to fall asleep—drift off into a darkness that I'd never wake from again. Perhaps this water would take me. It'd be ironic, really. A half-breed mermaid, killed by her own element.

Something drifted through the water, tickling my collar bone. I peeled my heavy eyes open and looked downward. It was the vial of ocean water and sand that I wore around my neck.

I pulled it from my chest to examine the water inside. Closing my eyes and taking a deep breath, I channeled my energy to my fingers. Logic told me I should open them and find the water swirling inside, but when I finally looked at the necklace, the water remained still.

I had lost my home, my family, my friends, and my magic—I'd lost *everything*.

The council said one day they may welcome me back, but without certainty of when that day may come, their promises were empty. The council said they were protecting me, but they hadn't even asked if I wanted to be protected. Danger of any sort felt like a welcome adversary compared to the numbness that had overtaken me.

The council couldn't save me. All they'd done was take everything from me without blinking an eye. So what could I do to save myself?

I'd made up my mind before I could finish asking the question.

I was going to get my magic back, even if that meant prying it from Carson's cold, dead fingers.

CHAPTER 10

I returned to the dorm room and got dressed. I didn't know what I was going to do, but I knew I had to get out of here. I still had the money my mom had given me, but the problem was I didn't have any transportation. Busses didn't go in or out of Sea Haven. A taxi ride would cost me a fortune. Would anyone even rent a car to me? And even if I could get a plane ticket, I didn't have any way to get from the airport back to Sea Haven. They weren't exactly within walking distance.

I glanced around the room as if I'd find an answer there. My eyes fell on the piece of paper Sharon had left on my dresser with her phone number.

Maybe she can help me, I wondered briefly, but I quickly shot that idea down. Sharon said she'd chosen to leave. She said she didn't feel the pull of the ocean as strongly, that it had faded over time. It didn't sound like she wanted to go back. Would she understand my desire to return, to reclaim what was mine? I didn't think she would.

Still, I needed a car—or someone with a car. I fell to the bed and buried my face in my hands. My mind played through the scenario I'd dreamt of only hours ago. I pictured walking up the steps of City Hall and confronting Carson. I imagined defeating him and taking my magic back. But it was all just a fantasy...

Something else flickered through my mind. In my dream, Noah Starr had stepped through the doors to City Hall and winked at me.

I shot straight up in bed. Noah was the last person I knew who'd left Sea Haven. Maybe his pull toward the ocean hadn't faded yet. Maybe he would understand my need to return. Maybe... maybe he was like me.

I reached for my phone. Noah and I had only ever spoken a handful of times. I wasn't friends with him, but it didn't take long to find his profile. The first thing I did was check his location, and hope surged through me. He lived in Chicago, which wasn't far. I could take a bus and meet up with him

Is this where they just drop us all off? I wondered. *As far from the ocean as they can?*

I told myself to stop thinking too hard and quickly sent Noah a message. *Hey! I know it's been a while, but I'm in*

Illinois. It's my first time out of Sea Haven, and I don't know anyone here. I was wondering if we could meet up.

As I waited for his reply, I scrolled through his profile. I smiled when I saw a picture of him fishing on a big lake. The smile on his face told me he missed the water. I reached a picture of him standing beside his new car. At least he had a car. Whether he'd go along with my suggestion or not was another question.

He didn't post often, so it didn't take long to reach a post from nearly a year ago that caught my eye. In it, he mentioned his new address in case anyone wanted to send him anything. I paused at the post for a minute, burning the address into my memory.

Curiously, I clicked on the comment section and scrolled through it. Several people I knew from Sea Haven had commented saying congratulations. It sounded like most admired him for leaving, like they didn't personally have the balls to do it themselves. I wouldn't have, either. It wasn't that I was scared of the outside world. Sea Haven had always been my home, and I didn't want to leave the people I loved. It was beautiful. Peaceful.

Or so I'd thought.

I rose angrily from the bed, that feeling of betrayal raging through my veins again. It momentarily struck me how this was the first time I'd ever been out of Sea Haven and I'd spent most of it cooped up in this room. I should have been outside exploring the world. But somehow, it didn't matter. All that mattered right now was Noah's reply. Was this guy going to help me get my magic back or not?

I glanced down at my phone as if somehow his reply would have come through in the last two seconds. It hadn't.

I waited all night for Noah's reply, but it never came. I woke the next morning with no notification from him.

I paced around the room. Hours must've passed, until I couldn't wait any longer.

I dropped to the floor and unzipped my suitcase. I pulled my pictures out of it and set them around the room where they fit best. Then, I transferred my clothes from my bag to the dresser. I didn't bother making the bed.

As a final touch, I situated a few notebooks on the desk and then tucked my empty suitcase into the closet—if you could even call it that. It was more of a cubby space with a rod for hanging clothes. It didn't even have a door on it.

I shoved what I could into my backpack. I double checked that the envelope of cash my mom had given me was still safely tucked into one of the front zippered pockets.

I glanced around the room. It looked enough like I'd settled in that if Sharon came to check on me, she might not notice me missing. Satisfied, I slung my bag over my shoulder and began toward the door. I checked my phone one last time to see if Noah had replied, but he hadn't yet.

Just as I went to tuck my phone back into my pocket, I paused. My paranoia came alive once again. They could be tracking me with GPS on my phone. It was better to be safe than sorry. If I was going to get my magic back, they couldn't know I was coming. I took four strides across the small room and slipped the phone into the top drawer of the desk.

As I turned away from it, my heart dropped. That was my only line of connection to Noah, and I was just going to leave it here?

Yes, because either way, I needed to see Noah in person.

Bus station, here I come.

CHAPTER 11

I resituated the backpack straps on my back when I stepped off the bus, then headed in the direction of Noah's address. I quickly found the building I was looking for and caught the door as a guy about my age exited the building.

Noah's apartment sat on the second floor, and it didn't take me long to find. I didn't knock right away, though. I stood outside the door and inhaled a deep breath, hoping I was doing the right thing. After a beat to collect myself and calm my racing heart, I placed my fist to the door and knocked.

A silent moment passed, leaving me to wonder if he was even home. Hope surged through my heart when I heard shuffling behind the door. The knob clicked, and then the door popped open a crack.

I recognized Noah behind it. He'd grown more muscular over the past year and had cut his hair since the last time I saw him at his high school graduation. The new style suited him well. I noticed a small amount of stubble across his jawline, which seemed stronger and more chiseled than I remembered. He seemed so much more grown up, like the world outside of Sea Haven had somehow changed him.

Noah stood with one shoulder behind the door as if using it for protection. Confusion crossed his face for a moment as if wondering who I was, and then recognition hit.

"I need your help," I spat out. Before he could get a word in, I tried again for a better introduction. "I'm sorry. Bree Waters. You probably don't remember me—"

"I remember you. I just... didn't expect to see you here."

"Did you get my message?" I asked.

"I don't get online much. I get homesick if I'm on there all the time. Too many people posting about home. Um... why don't you come in?" Noah opened the door wider to welcome me inside the small apartment.

After I stepped inside, Noah crossed his arms over his chest and leaned against the front door. "Why'd you come here, Bree?"

"Long story short..." I couldn't believe I was going for the *short* version. Usually, every story I told was the long version. "I was forced out of Sea Haven and stripped of my magic."

His brows furrowed for a moment, before he forced a laugh. "You must have really pissed someone off."

I could tell it was supposed to come off as a joke, but it sounded more like he was fishing for information.

"I didn't do anything wrong," I told him honestly. "They sent me away because Carson Ray is determined to make my life a living hell."

Noah laughed lightly, and the corners of his mouth twitched up into a near smile. I liked talking to someone who understood. After all the people I'd passed on my way here, the world outside of Sea Haven felt so foreign to me, and it was nice to be back in some familiar company. Noah and I had only had one class together in high school, but I knew he'd understand Sea Haven unlike anyone else. No one could ever forget a place like that.

"I'm here because I need your help," I said. "You're the last person I know who left Sea Haven, and I thought maybe you could help me get back."

As I glanced around the small space, I noticed two bedrooms, one off the living room near the bathroom and another near the tiny kitchen. "Do you have a roommate?"

The confusion in his eyes seemed to have settled some, though it hadn't completely disappeared. "I do, but he's not here right now."

I gave a sigh of relief and fell onto the couch next to

me. It sank in so far that I feared I'd never get back up, but I needed to sit down. "We're alone?"

Noah nodded, then shook his head in disbelief. "This is crazy. I never thought I'd see anyone from Sea Haven ever again. Yet here you are..."

How did he remain so calm? A girl from his hometown—one that was a secret from the world—comes knocking at his door, and he just goes along with it? He should be the one asking *me* questions. As soon as the thought crossed my mind, Noah began pacing around the small space. He raked his fingers through his hair.

This was a bad idea, I thought. *Maybe I shouldn't have come.* I almost stood and headed for the door, ready to let him live in peace without a reminder of home, but now that I was here, I couldn't leave. He was the most familiar thing I'd seen since leaving Sea Haven, and I wasn't ready to walk away from that just yet. That's not to mention I wasn't sure if I could get out of this couch anyway. It was practically eating me whole. I swear I was only a few inches from sitting on the floor by now.

His expression softened, and he came to sit on the coffee table across from me. He spoke softly. "They took your magic without your consent?"

I felt as if I was sinking deeper into the couch under his gaze. "Unfortunately."

"That's unfair." He let out a puff of air like he honestly couldn't process the concept.

I eyed him curiously. "Does that mean you gave up your magic voluntarily?"

His eyes moved just enough to call the motion an eye roll. "Technically, yes. It was go to school out here, or sit in a jail cell."

I was shocked to hear that. Noah didn't seem like the kind of guy to break the law. "What happened?"

"It was supposed to be a stupid senior prank," Noah said. "I got caught spray painting the old lighthouse."

"That's hardly a reason to send you away!" I cried.

Noah shrugged. "The council didn't think so. They slapped me with all these charges—vandalism, destruction of property... I don't even know the whole list. They thought sending me to school out here would help me or something. All they did was drop me here without any resources."

"They were wrong to do that," I insisted.

Noah dropped his gaze. "I needed to get away."

I could tell his words held a deeper meaning, and whatever happened was a really sensitive topic. I didn't want to prod. Instead, I asked, "Has the distance helped?"

He shook his head, but his expression remained stoic. Noah was difficult to read. "No, I think only time can do that."

"Would you go back if you could?" I wondered.

He gazed at a spot on the wall just above my head. "I'm not sure..." He held out the last word as if he had more to say, but he didn't finish.

I glanced around the room, and I noticed the fishing pole propped up in the corner, along with a tackle box on the counter. A conch shell sat on the bookcase, and a small saltwater fish tank bubbled next to the TV.

I leaned closer to Noah. "You still feel the pull of the ocean, don't you?"

"Of course I do," he said like it was a no-brainer. "I've been dying to step my toes in salt water since the day I left."

"You miss your magic," I stated.

"Every damn day."

"Then let's get it back," I whispered.

He paused for a beat, as if considering this, then pulled away from me. "I have school. I have a lease here. I can't just leave." He stood and ran his fingers through his hair again.

I got to my feet beside him. "Of course you can. To hell with all this!" I gestured around the apartment.

He shook his head. "I told myself I'd stay here for four years, finish my schooling. What does it matter to you if I go back or not?"

Silence hung in the air for a beat. I could hardly get the words out as my throat closed up. "Because I don't have any other way back. I'm alone, Noah. You're the only person who can help me."

Sympathy flashed across his face, but it faded when he crossed his arms over his chest. His voice filled with curiosity. "Why should I help you?"

My eyes locked on the fish swimming around in the tank as I considered my answer. Finally, I turned to him.

"Because we both want the same thing. We want our magic back, and this is the only way to do it—together."

He eyed me. "What's your plan, then? You said they took your magic from you without your consent. They're not just going to give it back."

"You're right. I can't just walk in and ask for it back. That's why we're going to steal it."

CHAPTER 12

Noah was desperate to return to Sea Haven. I could see it in his eyes. He longed for his magic as much as I did.

"What are we going to do after we get our magic back?" he asked while packing his things for the trip.

"We get in, get our magic, and get as far away from Sea Haven as possible," I told him. "Back to the ocean, of course, but not Sea Haven. Not anywhere near Carson Ray."

Or Dr. Sloan, I thought. I knew he was just following Carson's orders, but he'd been the one to physically take my magic, and that made him just as bad. I thought of my father briefly, how he'd played a role in it. I didn't want to be near him, either. Too bad that meant I'd have to distance myself from my mom and my friends as well. That was the last thing I wanted, but at least I'd have my magic, and I'd have the ocean until I figured out the rest.

Noah slung his bag over his shoulder and then turned to me, shaking his head.

"What?" I asked, straightening up from where I was leaning against his bedroom's door frame.

"I can't believe I'm going along with this. I barely know you."

I smiled slyly. "That's what makes it fun."

"This is crazy," he mumbled under his breath.

We exited his apartment, and Noah pulled his phone out. I noticed it was a cheap flip phone.

"What are you doing?" I asked.

"Texting my roommate. Letting him know I won't be around for a bit."

Noah led me to a parking garage and to a silver sedan I recognized from the picture I saw earlier. I noticed the car was beginning to rust around the wheel wells and looked to be a good decade old.

"You're paying for gas," he said as he clicked a button on his key fob to unlock the door.

"Not a problem." I eyed the car closer. "Are you sure this thing is going to make it?"

Noah opened his door. "She's reliable. I promise."

"Okay," I said skeptically as I slid into the passenger seat.

"You've got GPS?" he asked.

I bit down on my bottom lip. I'd left my phone—including the dummy one—in my dorm room so the council couldn't track me. "No," I admitted.

He rested his hands on the steering wheel. "You don't have a smartphone?"

"You don't, either. I have one; I just didn't bring it along."

"I guess we'll have to do it the old-fashioned way." Noah started the car and pulled out of the parking space. "We need gas anyway. I'm sure we can pick up a map at a gas station."

We must've been driving for hours in silence. I wanted to thank Noah for helping me, but every time I thought I might, my throat closed up, and I couldn't find the words. What could I possibly say to him? *Thank you* didn't seem like enough.

Just as I thought I'd found the words and opened my mouth to say something, Noah reached toward the radio but almost immediately turned the volume down. "Sorry. Were you going to say something?"

I knotted my hands in my lap. "I wanted to say thank you for helping me."

He glanced my way before fixing his gaze back on the road. "It's not fair what they did to us. We have to stick together."

The world was a big, big place. I'd only been away for a day and already I was beginning to understand how much bigger it was than I could have ever imagined. Of all the people in the world, less than twenty thousand resided in Sea Haven, which meant there weren't a lot of people like us left. The whole point of Sea Haven was to preserve our ancestry. People didn't come and go often because we needed to stick together. And now Noah and I had something bigger in common—we'd left.

He was right. We had to stick together no matter what.

"Why do you think they take our magic?" he asked thoughtfully. "Did they ever tell you?"

"They told me everything then took my magic against my will," I said sarcastically, before my voice turned serious again. "I think they wanted to punish me to keep me quiet."

"For what?" Noah asked curiously.

I gazed out the window.

"Well, I guess it worked," he said when I didn't answer.

I realized almost instantly he was right. "They said they take our magic so no one finds out about us, because if they did, they'd come for the whole town. I'm not sure I believe them. They don't tell you that you have to give up your magic to leave, until you do. I always thought we were free to go if we wanted."

"Maybe that's it," Noah suggested. "They make you think you want to stay, so you don't feel like a prisoner."

Prisoner. Is that what the residents of Sea Haven were? Was that the cost of keeping our secret from the rest of the world? Except if we were prisoners, why did they let us leave at all?

"You didn't tell anyone about giving up your magic after you left?" I asked curiously.

He shook his head. "I was under the impression I wasn't supposed to."

Silence hung in the air as we both digested his words.

"If we're going to drive through the night, we should probably trade off driving," I finally said. "Which means I should get some sleep. Wake me when you're too tired to keep driving, okay?"

I pulled one of the t-shirts I'd packed out of my bag, balled it up, and placed it between my head and the window to use as a pillow.

I barely slept. When my eyes adjusted to the darkness, I realized I was still seated in Noah's passenger seat. Checking the time on the clock, I noticed several hours had already passed. The gas gauge showed a full tank. Noah must've stopped at the gas station while I was asleep. He glanced my way.

A long yawn escaped his lungs when he spoke. "You're awake."

I sat straighter. "I guess I am now. Do you need me to drive?"

He shrugged. "It's either that or we stop for the night. Hotel's on you."

"Ha ha," I said sarcastically. "We can get there faster if I drive."

He raised a single brow and glanced over at me. "You sure? Driving these highways isn't the same as driving in town back home."

"You say that like I've never driven over thirty-five miles per hour before."

"What else am I supposed to think? It's not like you got out of Sea Haven much."

He wasn't wrong.

"My friend's grandparents live a couple miles out of town," I said. "The speed limit on their road is fifty-five."

"And these roads are faster," he stated simply.

"I'll be fine. I *do* have my driver's license," I added liked that proved something.

Silence stretched between us for a beat, but Noah kept his eyes on the road. "How far do you think the council would let you go with magic? Do you think it's just something they do for people who leave long-term?"

"What do you mean?" I asked.

"You said your friend's grandparents live a couple miles out of town. I knew a couple of people just on the outside of town, too. So, clearly the council is fine with that, but where do they draw the line? At the next town over? What if you want to go on vacation, just leave for a week or something? And what if you didn't tell them you were leaving? Would they even know?"

"You ask all this like you think I have an answer."

"No." He shook his head. "It's just something to ponder."

Silence filled the car again, and I noticed his eyes drooping.

"I can drive," I insisted. He seemed like he could use the sleep much more than I could.

"I'll stop at the next exit," he offered.

We didn't say much else. Eventually, I settled into the driver's seat while Noah reclined the passenger seat. I noticed the change in his breathing rate. It slowed within minutes, indicating he'd fallen asleep.

Noah was right when he'd said driving on these roads was different from driving back home. I felt like I was going too fast, but every time I checked the speedometer, I realized I was driving below the speed limit. I found the cruise control and settled in for a long ride.

Eventually, the sun began to peek over the edge of the horizon behind us. Noah stirred in his seat.

"What's up, sleepy head?" I reached over to turn off the quiet tunes I'd been playing on the radio.

Noah yawned, then situated his seat into the upright position and stared out the window at the dark sky that stretched in front of us. "How far away are we?"

"We're over halfway, but we won't get there until tonight," I said.

"And what happens when we get there?" Noah asked. "Do you *have* a plan?"

My hands tightened on the steering wheel. "I'm figuring it out as I go."

"You haven't thought this through at all," he stated.

"You say that like you know me, but you don't."

The leather of his seat squeaked as he resituated himself to face me. "Then maybe we should get to know each other."

I glanced at him, then quickly turned my face away. "What do you want to know?"

He shrugged. "You're an only child?"

I nodded. "You?"

"Yeah."

Well, there was another thing we had in common.

"Sometimes I wished I had siblings, though, you know?" he asked.

I twisted my face up. "I don't know. My friend Liana has three brothers. It sounds awful."

Noah laughed again. The sound felt so strange to my ears. With everything that happened recently, it didn't seem like we should be laughing. It felt like we should be screaming.

"Oh, come on," he pleaded, noticing my frown. "We have a lot of time to kill. Might as well enjoy it."

I didn't think I could. One second, it almost felt like I could laugh along with him. The next, Carson crossed my mind, and all I wanted to do was punch the guy in the face. Or crotch.

I raised a challenging eyebrow. "Okay. Tell me more about yourself."

"You have to play the game, too."

I didn't meet his eyes. Instead, my gaze locked on the road in front of me. The sun was beginning to brighten the sky more, but the endless landscape in front of me made it feel like we weren't getting any closer to our goal.

I sighed heavily. "Fine. But you have to ask the questions, and I'm allowed to not answer if I don't want to."

When I glanced over at him, one corner of his mouth had turned down, but he agreed to play along. "First question. Is it true that you were the one who put the goldfish in the pool at school my senior year?"

"Pass."

He let out a breath of air and sat up straighter in his chair, as if I was being unfair. "You're going to pass on everything I ask, aren't you?"

"Pass." I couldn't help it when the corners of my lips twitched, resisting a smile.

"How about you only get one pass? Are you sure you want to use it up on this question?"

"Pass." The more I annoyed him, the more I felt my smile grow.

He narrowed his eyes at me.

"Fine," I caved. "Yes, I was an accomplice. So sue me."

"That was cruel, you know?"

I glanced sideways at him. Of course, he had to remind me. "How was I supposed to know all the fish would be dead the next day and the janitor would have to scoop them all out? It's not like it was my idea. I only tagged along with a group of senior guys."

"Didn't you toilet paper the gym a week later?" he asked, and I visibly blushed. "That one must've been your idea."

"Weren't you saying something about a plan?" I asked to change the subject.

"Oh, come on," he said with amusement. "I want to

hear all about the other badass things you've done. Which one was it that got you sent away?"

Silence filled the car as Noah awaited my response.

"You're not going to believe me," I finally said.

He leaned back in his chair. "Try me."

Memories rushed back. First, Tristan's blue-green eyes. Then the surprise on my mother's face when she found out how soon I was leaving. Then the weight of my father holding me down so they could steal my magic.

"I found a merman washed ashore," I told him.

"A merman... like me?" He spoke slowly, choosing his words carefully.

I shook my head. "A merman, like one of our ancestors —tail and everything."

"That's not possible," Noah insisted.

"And yet here we are. The council says he's dangerous, and that they sent me away because he'd come after me. If he does, so be it. At least with my magic, I'd stand a fighting chance."

"Your magic won't stand a chance against a merman. Are you *sure* he had a tail?"

"As sure as I am talking to you now," I said. "The merfolk didn't die off like we thought. They're still out there, and we don't know if he's bringing others. But if he is, I can't be on the other side of the country while my family and friends fight them off. I won't walk away from them."

"So, how do we get our magic back? We can't just waltz in there."

"It's not exactly a high security prison," I pointed out.

"If I remember right, there's a keypad on the door." Sarcasm dripped from his tone.

"I know the code," I stated confidently.

"And what about the lock?"

I shrugged. "We bust it. Pick it. Something."

Noah nodded slowly. "Right. I don't know how to pick a lock. You?"

"You'd think so, but no. Couldn't we just shoot the doorknob like they do in movies?"

He cocked an eyebrow. "And where are you getting a gun? How are we going to get in unnoticed?"

"It's not like City Hall is heavily guarded," I pointed out.

"No, but there are security cameras and alarm systems. If we want to get in and out without alerting anyone, we're going to need a key. Your dad works for the council, doesn't he?"

"Yeah, but he doesn't have a key to City Hall, and even if he did, he doesn't have one to that room. Dr. Sloan was the one with the key."

"Then we have to target him. If we can get his keys, then we can get in and out of City Hall without tripping the alarms. Then we'd be long gone with our magic before anyone did inventory and noticed they were missing."

"So instead of breaking and entering to get our magic, you want to break and enter to find the key? It adds another unnecessary step," I pointed out.

"Do you want them to notice our magic missing right

away?" Noah asked with a raised eyebrow. "Because broken windows and door handles will do that. A missing set of keys will keep them guessing if they don't know we're back in town. Getting our hands on Dr. Sloan's keys should be easy."

I narrowed my eyes at him. "Where are you going with this?"

"Doesn't your mom work with Dr. Sloan?"

My initial knee-jerk reaction was to slam on the brakes for him even *suggesting* it, but I thought better of it. "No way. We are *not* getting my mom involved in this. That's one of the reasons I went along with all this in the first place. I didn't want my mom or my friends to get hurt. If the council finds out she helped, they'll take her magic and send her away, too—or worse." I was sure of it.

"That's the beauty of the plan, though. No one will be suspicious. Besides, you didn't really think you could walk into Sea Haven without getting your family and friends involved, did you?"

I swallowed hard. He was probably right about that, but I couldn't bear to think of what the council would do to my mom if I got her involved. Would they strip her of her magic and send her away like they did to me? I couldn't let that happen.

"Not my mom, okay?" My voice came out sounding small.

I could see Noah's lips turn down from out of the corner of my eye.

"Fine," he agreed. "We won't get your mom involved."

I didn't know who I could drag into this—or who I should. The only person I thought I could turn to would be my father since he was already a part of it, but that didn't seem right. He'd just hand me over to Carson and send me away again—or more likely, lock me in one of the rooms in their basement like they'd done to Tristan.

"If we're going to steal Dr. Sloan's keys, we need to buy ourselves another day," I said. "By the time we get there, it will be dark, and we'll need a place to crash in the meantime."

He must've noticed the implication in my voice. "Who are we turning to for help?"

I hated this part. I didn't even want to say it out loud, as if that would mean I was committed to bringing someone else into this. But I didn't know where else to go, or where else to hide.

Liana was the only person I completely trusted. With how many sleepovers we'd held over the years—one almost every other weekend since kindergarten—and the many, *many* secrets I'd told her during those sleepovers, she'd never breathed a word of my secrets to a soul. And I knew she would be able to keep this one a secret.

I just hoped it didn't get her hurt.

CHAPTER 13

My heart hammered uncontrollably. Noah's breathing was so loud behind me that I was sure he was going to wake the neighborhood. I glanced around the street, praying no one would spot us.

We'd parked Noah's car outside of town down a dead-end road. If the rust on the wheel wells didn't give us away, his Illinois license plate would.

We walked into town at a swift pace. The closer we got to the ocean, the more excited I became. I could feel the ocean in the air, smell its familiar saltiness. I longed to bathe in the water and feel the waves rushing across my skin. It would have to wait.

Noah and I twisted through the streets of Sea Haven, avoiding streetlights whenever possible, until we were nearly to the ocean.

I could hear the waves now, crashing against the sand and rocks behind my house. It was all so familiar, so comfortable. And that itself felt wrong.

I could see my house from here. It wasn't too far down the beach from Liana's house, but I knew I wouldn't make it that far. I wasn't here to chew out my father, or to cry into my mother's arms. I was here for my magic, and that was it.

I slipped around the side of Liana's house, Noah right behind me, and inched my way over to her window. We'd knocked at each other's windows plenty of times throughout the years, and we even had a secret knock. Two knocks with your knuckle. One scratch across the window with your fingernails. One more knock.

I crouched next to the house and glanced up and down the beach one last time, before knocking on the window.

The only sounds came from the familiar lapping of the waves on shore and Noah's breath behind me. I glanced behind me at the waves. We were only yards away, yet it felt like miles.

I swallowed the lump in my throat and knocked on the window again. There was a ninety-nine percent chance Liana was asleep. I could either give up or pry her window open. I was weighing my options when, to my surprise, the window opened a crack.

Liana's voice hissed from behind it in a whisper. "Bree? What are you doing here? I thought you—"

Before she could finish her thought, I began making my way through the small opening into her bedroom. My backpack caught on the window at first, but I flattened myself onto my belly and made it through. I ended up in a heap on her floor.

"I'll explain in a minute," I whispered back as Noah crawled through.

Liana's tired eyes widened. Her gaze flickered between Noah and me. "Whaaa..." She couldn't even manage to get the full word out.

I dropped my backpack off my shoulders and stood. Noah set his bag next to mine.

"You're probably going to want to sit down for this," I advised Liana.

She leaned against one of her canopy posts to steady herself as she lowered herself to the bed. "I—I thought you left."

"I did," I stated simply.

Her eyes remained wide and unblinking. They drifted from me to Noah, slower this time than before. Another sweep back to Noah, and her gaze locked on him.

"You're Noah Starr," she said in a quiet voice.

He nodded.

Liana spoke slowly. "So you both left... and now..."

"And now we're back," Noah finished for her.

"And we need your help," I added.

We explained everything to Liana in the half hour that

followed. I told her about how I'd found Tristan on the beach, and how the council had taken my magic before they sent me away.

Liana shook her head in disbelief. "I'm so sorry this is all happening to you both. I'll help any way I can. I just wish you didn't have to leave again."

"I don't want to, but until the council deems it safe, they're not going to let me stay," I told her.

"I'm glad you're back," she said. "I thought I wouldn't see you again for a long time. It makes sense now. It seemed so unlike you to decide something so big without talking to me about it first. But I guess there's a side of you that might actually run off like that."

She was right about that one. Maybe that's why my friends and family just went along with it, because I *would* be the type of person to jump on a big decision like that in a snap. But seriously? Journalism? They should have known something was up when I mentioned that.

"I hate dragging you into this," I admitted. "We just need a place to hang out for a bit. If things go as planned, we'll be long gone before they realize what we did. No one will know you helped us."

Liana eased herself back down onto the bed and glanced between me and Noah. "What exactly is your plan?"

"We need keys so we don't trip the alarms in City Hall," Noah said. "I suggested getting Bree's mom to help us get Dr. Sloan's keys. She won't let her mom get involved, though."

"It's bad enough asking Liana for help," I said. "At least if we get caught, she can still plead the innocent little girl card. My mom wouldn't be able to get away with that."

Liana tilted her head and batted her eyes. "You think I'm an innocent little girl? How cute!"

I smirked. "Let's be honest. You have more balls than my mom does."

Liana shot a nervous glance at the door. "Shh... We don't want to wake anyone. As long as you two stay quiet, you can hang out here. My family never comes into my room. If you're going to steal Dr. Sloan's keys, then you have to be careful. What if I stole them?"

"What are you thinking?" I asked.

"I could visit your mom at the clinic, use her as an excuse to get in," she said with a shrug.

I pressed my lips together. "That'll spark suspicion. You've never visited her before."

"I think we're missing something," Noah said. "It's not just about getting into the clinic or distracting him. We know he has the keys, but we don't know where he keeps them. He might not even keep the key to City Hall and the key to the door we need in the same place. They could be at home, at his office, or on him."

"That's three options," I pointed out. "There are three of us. Liana can take Dr. Sloan—fake an emergency illness and ask to see him."

She nodded along, like it was a good idea. "What am I going to fake?"

"I remember my mom talking about this kid who came

in once complaining about finger pain. They didn't think anything was wrong until they took the X-rays and found out he'd fractured one of the bones in his finger. You couldn't even tell looking at it. I think that would be a good one. You were in the high school play freshman year. I know you have the acting chops to pull this off. Just remember to keep an eye out for his keys. The one to the door we need is a small golden key. And the one for City Hall is silver and shaped like an ocean wave."

"I'll take his office," Noah offered.

"That leaves me with his home," I said.

"Then it's settled." Liana stood and crossed the room over to her closet and dug out two sleeping bags. "You're lucky we still have these from our sleepover days."

Noah situated himself at the foot of Liana's bed, so I took the spot beside it near the door. As soon as I lay down, my face stretched into a yawn. It didn't matter that the floor was hard and uncomfortable. I was exhausted. I just wanted to go to sleep and wake up to reality.

Unfortunately, I was going to have to accept that this was my new reality.

CHAPTER 14

Darkness enveloped me.

"Noah!" I cried. My feet dangled below me as I gripped the edge of a cliff. I made the mistake of glancing to the waters below me. The ocean waves crashed against the rock violently. Water sprayed in my direction as if the waves were the teeth of a sea beast ready to swallow me whole.

"Noah!" I cried again. I didn't know how I knew it, but I knew he was at the top of the cliff somewhere.

"It's okay," Noah said softly. I looked upward to see him gazing down at me.

I locked eyes on his face, not wanting to look down toward the raging water again. "Help me! I'm slipping."

He lay on his belly and reached out toward me over the edge of the cliff. The closer his fingers reached toward mine, the farther away they seemed.

"I can't fall. I won't be able to breathe!" Not to mention that the waves and rock would probably crush me.

"Reach out to me!" he called back over the roaring wind.

"I can't!" My fingers grew weak with each passing moment.

"Just reach up and grab my hand. Trust me. It will be okay."

My body shook, but the sincerity in his voice made it easier to trust him. Steeling my nerves, I released my right-hand grip on the rock and used the last of my energy to pull up with my left fingers, just far enough to reach Noah's outstretched hand.

He pulled. I was surprised at how light I felt. Before I could truly process it, I was lying on solid ground. Noah's face hovered above mine, and he panted softly.

"See?" he asked, brushing a strand of hair out of my eyes. "I told you that you could trust me."

I awoke to the sunlight seeping in through the window. It was warm and welcoming. The sound of the ocean waves past the window reached my ears, and a painful longing for the water hit my gut.

Noah shifted at the foot of the bed. The thought of him brought back memories of my dream, and my face heated.

I shouldn't be feeling this way, I told myself. *I barely know Noah.*

My mind seemed settled on that argument, but minutes later when Noah sat up, his hair in disarray, I couldn't help my heart from pattering hard against the side of my rib cage. He'd saved me in the dream... just as he had helped me now.

"Okay, guys." Liana's voice surprised me. I jerked my head in her direction and found her at the door instead of her bed as I expected. She must've woken and stepped over me while I was still asleep.

"My family is in the kitchen getting ready for breakfast. If you need to use the bathroom, now's your chance."

I groaned and sat up straight. "I guess I'll go first."

I snuck down the hall. When I returned to her room, Liana had laid out several granola bars and a few apples on her bed.

"Breakfast is served," she said with a smile.

"Thanks." I picked up an apple and bit into it.

Noah crossed the room and tiptoed out of it toward the bathroom.

"Do you want to listen to the show?" Liana's smile transformed. It was still a smile, sure, but it was unmistakably an evil one.

"The show?" I asked.

"I have to put on a show if my injury is going to sound believable."

I nodded slowly like I understood. I didn't. Not really.

"I just have to get one of my brothers riled up." She bit the end of her lip and crinkled her nose up as if she had an evil little plan. It sure sounded like she did. "Just watch—er, listen. It'll be fun. I just have to wait for Noah to come back."

Noah returned a minute later.

"Liana's going to put on a show," I said casually from my spot on her bed. I bit into the final bite of my apple.

"You two have to be quiet in here, okay?" Liana warned as she hopped up from the bed.

We both nodded.

Liana tossed her blond hair over her shoulder and turned to us with one hand on the doorknob. "This is going to be fun!"

Noah took a seat next to me on the bed and picked up one of the granola bars between us. Besides the crinkle of the wrapper, the room remained silent. I locked my attention on the sounds outside the door. Voices drifted from the other end of the house as Liana's family chattered around the breakfast table. Then the sound of Liana flushing the toilet reached my ears. The door to the bathroom creaked open, and I heard the slap of her feet against the hardwood floor as she retreated down the hall.

"Gross!" she shouted so the entire house could hear.

"Which one of you left a giant hair ball in the drain this morning?"

I turned to Noah. "Which one do you think she's going to get? Taylor or Tyler?"

"Those her brothers?" he asked while he chewed.

I nodded. "The twins. They're two years younger than her."

"And her other brother's Lucas, right? From my grade? Or were they cousins?"

"Lucas is her older brother. He doesn't live here anymore, though."

One of the twins' voices carried down the hall. "It wasn't me!"

"Me, either," the other one said.

I couldn't tell which was which. Their voices were almost more identical than their faces.

"This is the last time I'm cleaning it out for you." Liana's voice seemed more distant now. I guessed she had already reached the kitchen.

One of the twins laughed loudly. Their arguments always seemed to turn their voices up about twice where they should be. The sound of Liana bickering with her brothers was surprisingly soothing. It felt familiar.

"It was you, wasn't it, Tyler?" Liana accused.

"You're the one with the most hair," one of the twins accused. "It's probably all yours anyway."

I pictured Liana narrowing her eyes and placing her hands on her hips like she did most times she argued with them.

"Your hair is as long as mine—both of yours," she countered.

"Will you kids simmer down?" her mom said so calmly that I could hardly make out the words.

"I'm sick of being the one to clean up after these two around here," Liana cried.

I heard her father mutter something back, but I couldn't make it out.

"Stop blaming us," one of the boys said. I pictured him sticking his tongue out at her. For teenagers, you'd think they would have grown out of childish teasing like that, but they hadn't.

"Shut up," Liana bit back.

"No."

"Shut up."

"No."

Her parents' attempts to calm the situation got lost in the shuffle of voices.

"Shut up!"

"Make me."

"Oh, I'll make you."

That's when the true chaos erupted. The sound of shuffling feet echoed throughout the house. Liana yelled incomprehensible insults at her brother as he screamed at the top of his lungs. The pounding of their feet made their way through the living room and then the den before coming dangerously close to the door Noah and I sat behind.

On their way back toward the kitchen, a loud thud

came, the sound of a falling body. Liana cried out in pain. If I didn't know she was only acting, I would have been concerned myself. She shouted a few curses in her brother's direction, but other than that, the house had gone silent.

Noah and I exchanged a glance.

"Tyler!" Liana's mother scolded. "What did you do to your sister?"

Tyler sounded honestly concerned. "I didn't mean to! It wasn't my fault."

"Sure, it wasn't," Liana bit at him sarcastically. She sucked in long breaths that hissed between her teeth.

"Let me see." Her mother's voice carried down the hall.

"No," Liana cried. "It hurts too much."

"What happened?" her mom demanded.

"She ran into the door frame," Tyler explained, sounding horrified.

"Yeah, because I slipped on *your* sweat that you smeared all across the floor because you won't change your stupid stinky socks."

"They're not stinky! You're stinky." The concern had fled from his voice.

Noah smirked at me. "See, wouldn't it be fun to have siblings?"

My brows shot up. "I don't know if this sounds like fun."

"I think when we have kids—"

"Whoa," I stopped him before he could finish his

thought. The way he ordered his words caught me completely off guard.

"Oh, God, no," he laughed.

What did *that* mean?

"I meant our generation," he said. "I kind of want a lot. That way they'll have siblings, and once I get my magic back, I can pass it down to them—"

The bedroom door swung open, interrupting him. Both of us jumped at the sound of it, but we relaxed when seeing it was only Liana.

A wide grin was plastered on her face. "Stage one, complete."

CHAPTER 15

"What now?" I asked.

Liana waved her hand. "I'll go back out there before they all leave and complain that it still hurts. My parents will be leaving for work soon, and then my brothers will head down to the beach like they do every day. They're usually not back until dark. You're free to use the shower after everyone leaves."

"You didn't hurt yourself for real, did you?" Noah asked.

"Nah. I did punch the door frame—had to make it look real—but it only hurt for a minute. No broken bones." She held her hand up and wiggled her fingers to prove it. "I'll be right back."

Liana put herself back in character and stepped out of her room. She tiptoed down the hall with uneven steps and added a groan of pain for the show.

"You okay, sweetie?" her mother asked from the kitchen.

"I don't know," Liana said in a groggy voice. "It really hurts."

"Should we take you to the emergency room?" Her mother's voice filled with concern.

"No. I think I just need to put some ice on it. I can go to the doctor's myself if it doesn't stop throbbing in the next hour or so."

I could sense the hum of the freezer as Liana opened it for ice. She returned another minute later with two bottled waters and an ice pack she didn't need. She handed us each a water.

"Is your mom going to come in and check on you?" Noah asked.

"Nah, it's fine. She gives me my space when I need it."

It seemed like hours waiting for her family to leave the house, but it was only another half hour before we were alone.

I crept down the hall. It didn't feel right to be sneaking around like this, and I was suddenly afraid I'd be caught. I knew it was a silly fear; Liana's family would be gone all day, but my senses became heightened as if I thought someone would round the corner and spot me.

Once I stepped into the shower, my nerves began to ease. I set the water to cold and began to scrub down. The cool temperature felt refreshing on my skin. It reminded me of the ocean. The thought sent a twisting sensation to settle in my gut. Just yards away, beyond the confines of this wall, the ocean water was lapping ashore. Not much farther down the beach, everyone was beginning to gather in the calm waters for their daily swim. If only I could be out there with them. If only none of this ever happened. I thought about where I'd be if that were the case. I'd probably be right here in Liana's house, only for different reasons. We'd be planning for our college dorm and talking about hot guys on TV while we prepared to head down to the beach.

A knock came at the door, startling me. The hair on my arms stood, and not because of the chilly water. I froze, afraid it was one of Liana's family members.

"You almost done in there?" Noah's voice called through the door.

I relaxed, and the hairs on my arms fell back to their normal position. "Yeah, I'm almost done."

After rinsing myself a final time, I climbed out of the shower and dried myself down. At the mirror, I noticed for the first time how worn out I looked. My eyes seemed dark and sunken in, and my lips turned down into an involuntary frown.

I realized for the first time that I hadn't brought any extra clothes into the bathroom with me. I had no other choice but to wrap a towel around myself.

In the hall, Noah was waiting outside the door for his turn with the shower. His gaze darted downward, but he quickly looked away, and his expression remained neutral. I ducked my head and hurried toward Liana's room.

Liana turned from her mirror when I entered. "What are you blushing about?"

I raised my head and did my best to relax my face. "What? I wasn't blushing?" The lie was evident in my tone.

"Jeez," she teased, standing. "Put on some clothes."

She picked a t-shirt up from the pile on top of her dresser and tossed it my way. I caught the shirt in one hand and threw it back at her as she left the room to give me privacy.

I dug into my bag and found a clean set of clothes. Once fully dressed, I knotted the towel around my head to help dry my long hair.

"I'm done," I announced, and Liana reentered the room. "Do you mind if I use some of your makeup?" I turned to her desk and picked up a tube of mascara.

Liana knitted her brows as she returned to sit in front of her mirror to finish her makeup. "Why do you need makeup? No one's going to see you." A split second later, her expression relaxed. "Well, except for Noah."

I didn't like the teasing tone to her voice. Most of the time the teasing was familiar and comforting. But this? Accusing me of wanting to impress Noah? That was just *so* wrong.

"Don't even go there," I warned as she handed me her

foundation. "I'd like some makeup for myself, thank you very much. I certainly don't care what Noah thinks about me."

Liana looked uncertain. "You sure about that?"

I honestly *wasn't* sure. I pushed the idea out of my mind as quickly as it entered it.

"Yes, I'm sure." I turned to the mirror, ignoring her stare.

Noah returned to the bedroom, and Liana called to make an appointment with Dr. Sloan. After she hung up, she handed a navy-blue baseball cap in my direction.

"What's that for?"

"It's to keep people from recognizing you. Don't worry. Noah gets one, too." She handed him a gray cap. "And I have a couple pairs of sunglasses in the car."

I situated the cap on my head. "Let's do this."

Liana led us to the car in the garage. It was her mom's car, but her parents carpooled downtown for work most days.

She handed me the keys. "My appointment will take a while. You drop us off at the clinic and meet us back there."

I nodded. "Got it."

I started the car and backed out of the garage. A thick layer of clouds covered the sun, and the horizon was invisible through an overcast haze.

I passed by familiar houses, which brought back the comfort of home. As quick as the comfort came, it was replaced with a sinking feeling. As much as I felt like I was back home, I had to stop thinking of it that way. This wasn't my home anymore.

I dropped Liana and Noah off at the clinic.

"Good luck," Liana said.

"Here." Noah handed me his phone.

I took it. "What's this for?"

"In case you need to contact us," he said simply. "I already put Liana's number in."

"Thanks," I said. "I had her number memorized ages ago. I'll see you guys soon." I slipped the phone into my pocket.

They disappeared into the clinic, and I drove the few blocks to Dr. Sloan's house. It was one of the biggest in town, but crime was so low in Sea Haven that we had no need for security cameras. I didn't think I'd ever heard of a break-in here my whole life.

I parked the car a few houses down, then snuck around the side of the house. At the back of the house, I swallowed hard as I approached the sliding glass door. My heart hammered when I reached out toward the golden handle. The metal felt strangely cold on my sweaty hands. I slid the door open with ease and tiptoed into a vast room. The dining room table stood straight in front of me, and past that, the tile was interrupted by a layer of carpet, which housed a couch on one end of the room and a TV on the other. To my right stood a flight of stairs that led to the second level of the house, and on my left lay a kitchen complete with stainless steel appliances and an island separating the dining area from the kitchen area.

Past that, a hallway stretched back into the rest of the house.

If I were Dr. Sloan, I'd probably leave my keys in my bedroom. My best bet for that was either up the stairs or down the hall. I took my first step toward the hall when I heard a high-pitched squeak, like a sneaker against tile, come from that direction.

Instinct overcame me, and I immediately dropped to my knees and hurried across the floor behind the island. I held my breath as I pressed my back up against the cool wood of the kitchen cabinet. I exhaled slowly as to not make a sound and listened intently, my attention focused down the hall. Only silence met my ears. I let my full breath out and inhaled another one in relief.

After another moment of silence, I turned and gripped the edge of the counter to pull myself up. It was only when I straightened up and was about to take another step that I heard another sound. Immediately, I dropped to the floor again. This time, the rhythmic pattern of footsteps echoed down the hall. I held my breath again, and my heart thumped so hard against the sides of my chest that my whole body began to shake. I quickly glanced around in search of a way out, but I wouldn't reach the door in time, and there were no obvious hiding spots in sight. The footsteps only grew louder on their way to the kitchen.

Dr. Sloan is going to catch me, I thought. *This time, he'll do much worse to me.*

As long as I calculated this right and had a bit of luck on my side, I might be able to get away unseen.

The footsteps finally reached the kitchen, and so did the sound of a woman's breathing. The refrigerator hummed as the woman opened the door. I *really* didn't like how close I was to her. If I stayed where I was, she'd spot me. In the quietest move I could make, I crawled around the side of the island so I was facing the dining room table.

"Hmm..." the woman mused.

I didn't know the voice off-hand, but it had to be Dr. Sloan's wife.

What did she do for work, again? I racked my brain trying to remember. My mom had mentioned her once or twice, but I couldn't remember the details. Wasn't it something in health care? Was she a nurse or something? I hadn't anticipated anyone would be home this time of day.

I heard her cross the kitchen toward the sink. If I'd stayed where I was just moments ago, she would have surely caught me. The sound of running water filled the kitchen as she lifted the faucet handle. I was thankful for this bit of noise since it helped mask the sound of me shuffling around the corner of the island. Now I sat on the side closest to the hall. If I could only cross the last few feet unnoticed, I could find a better hiding spot in the next room.

Slowly, I leaned toward the edge of the cabinets. In the reflection of the stove, I saw she was facing away from me and washing something at the sink. I poked my head out further to peek around the side of the island. As she dropped the item she was holding into a small blue lunch bag, I realized it was an apple. She turned from the sink, and I instinctively pulled back. I heard her make her way toward the kitchen table, and I rounded the last corner of the island so I sat right next to the fridge.

Something jingled from across the room—the sound of keys. In the next moment, her footsteps became quiet when she stepped onto the carpet. The sound of the front door clicking shut reached my ears, and for the first time since entering the house, I breathed audibly. It was a long, refreshing breath, but it still felt like I wasn't getting enough oxygen to my lungs. What if she came back? What if someone else was in the house?

I didn't let myself think on it for long. All I knew was that in this moment, I had my chance to escape the wide-open space and get to a place where I had less of a chance of being spotted. I crossed the floor hastily, crawling at first, and then getting to my feet and shuffling down the hall. I slipped into the first door on the right—the bathroom—and ducked behind the open door, pressing myself between it and the wall.

I must've remained behind that door slowing my breathing and clutching the doorknob for a good ten minutes. My eyes stayed closed, by my ears remained on full alert, listening for other noises throughout the house. For as long as I waited there, the only thing I heard was my own breathing, the hum of the appliances, and the occasional car passing by outside. Each car I heard sent off alarm bells in my body. I listened intently to see if any would pull into the driveway, but none did.

Once I finally decided it was safe, I let the tension in my shoulders relax and stepped out from behind the door.

I slipped out of the bathroom and tiptoed down the hall. The next door on the right was a laundry room, and I didn't think I'd find anything in there. I continued down the hall to the door on my left. Peeking around the corner, I spotted a king-sized bed opposite a large closet and next to a door leading to another bathroom. Two nightstands stood on either side of the bed, and on opposite sides of the room, mirroring each other, were two long dressers.

I started at the dresser closest to the door. Only picture frames sat on top, so I couldn't tell who it belonged to. When I opened the top drawer, the women's clothing told me the dresser was Dr. Sloan's wife's. I closed the drawer quietly and rounded the bed to the long cherry-colored dresser at the other end of the room.

Opening the first drawer, I found a pile of neatly folded button-down shirts like the type my dad wore to work. I closed that drawer and tried another. All I found in each of the six drawers were clothes—no drawer of junk like I had in my dresser back home.

Glancing around the room in search of my next target, my gaze fell upon the bedside table closest to me. I opened the top drawer, holding my breath in anticipation, but the drawer was nearly empty save for a few books. I read the titles on each, but they sounded like boring doctor stuff.

I closed the drawer in disappointment and continued searching, moving over to the other bedside table, which was clearly on Mrs. Sloan's side of the room. I figured it didn't hurt to look, but I didn't find anything.

I turned to the closet. The door slid open easily on its tracks, opening to reveal a wall of neck ties. On the other end of the closet hung a row of Mrs. Sloan's dresses. I ignored that side and glanced up and down Dr. Sloan's side of the closet. A row of shoes lined the floor, but as far as I could tell, there was nowhere inside worth keeping a key.

A *thud* in the next room sent me back into fight-or-flight mode. I chose flight and immediately dropped to the floor next to the bed. Glancing around to form an exit strategy, I noticed quickly that I only had one option. I squeezed myself under the bed. The corners of the metal frame dug into my shoulder blade. Carpet scratched my exposed belly as my shirt rode up. There wasn't much room, but I managed to wiggle my way under the bed. There was just enough space between the edge of the comforter and the carpet that I could just barely see a sliver of the room from where I lay.

Small, soft footsteps padded down the hall, quickening my heart rate the closer they came.

Someone was going to catch me.

CHAPTER 16

I relaxed when a black and white cat entered the room, purring loudly. It didn't notice me as it jumped up onto the bed to lay down.

I let my forehead rest on the floor in relief. I only had a moment to enjoy how lucky I was before I went into full panic mode again. The phone in my pocket vibrated. It sounded like a fire alarm in the silence. There wasn't much room between the floor and the bed, so even with my tailbone pressed tightly against the underside of the box spring, I had to wedge my hand between my hip and the floor. At the same time, I attempted to twist my head around to my right, but there wasn't much room for that, either. Pinching the phone between my middle and index finger, I finally got it out of my pocket. Liana's name flashed across the screen, and I answered it quickly.

"What?" I hissed in a low whisper. Though I was sure I only had to worry about the cat, I didn't want to take my chances.

Liana's voice came over the line. "Found anything yet?"

"No," I said. "You?"

"I just saw Dr. Sloan. My exam isn't done, but when he stepped out of the room, I caught a glimpse of Noah leaving his office. He gave me a thumbs up, but I think he only got the key to City Hall. I don't think he got the key to the room your magic is in."

"I'll keep looking," I told her. "I'm putting the phone on silent until I'm done. You almost scared the crap out of me!"

"Now *that* would be funny," she teased.

"Not funny. Dr. Sloan's wife was here when I got here. I almost got caught!"

Liana drew in a sharp breath. "Oh, my gosh! I didn't even think of that. I thought she'd be at work."

"It's not your fault," I said. "I'll call you back if I find anything."

I hung up and clicked the button on the side to mute the ringtone. I paused for another moment to listen again for signs of life in the house. The only sound came from the cat purring loudly from above me.

I reached out from under the bed to try to wiggle

myself out. Before I made it halfway, a shadow in the corner caught my eye. I had to do a double take to confirm there was actually something under the bed. There definitely was something there, but what was it?

Pushing myself back under the bed, I reached out to grip the small dark cube. Pulling it closer to me, the sliver of light filtering in under the corner of the comforter showed it was a small metal container about the size of a shoe box. Heart pounding and fingers quivering, I slowly opened the top. Its metal hinges squeaked in a high pitch.

Inside, I found what looked mostly like junk. The contents were probably important to Dr. Sloan, but most people would only throw this stuff away. Old photographs sat on one side, each one stacked nicely on top of each other. The other side was full of old pieces of lined notebook paper, each note folded as neatly as the pictures were stacked.

On top of the pile of notes sat a key. Could this be the one? I couldn't tell in the dim lighting under the bed.

Sliding my body along the carpet again, I pulled myself out from under the bed, the box still in my hands. In the light, I could make out the shape and color of the key better, and my excitement flared.

"Yes!" I exclaimed before covering my mouth with my hand. I listened closely, but the house remained silent.

The black and white cat on the bed glared at me as if to ask who I was, where I came from, and what I was doing in his house.

I returned my attention to the box and key. This was

the key I'd seen Dr. Sloan use to get into the room. I was certain of it. I slipped the key into my pocket, then closed the box and slid it under the bed where I'd found it.

I stood and hurried down the hall. Just before I reached the end, I slowed and listened again to my surroundings. The sound of another car passed the house.

To my relief, the car continued down the road. Satisfied that I was alone, I crossed the kitchen to the back sliding glass doors, keeping low the entire way in case I needed to hit the floor again and hide. I managed to slip out the back unnoticed, my heart pounding the entire way.

Pulling my hat low on my head to shield my face, I hurried back to the car. I pulled Noah's phone out of my pocket again and checked to see if Liana had called or texted again after I turned the phone to silent.

Got it, I messaged Liana.

The sound of the vehicle sounded like a siren to my ears. I shot a glance up and down the street, but there was no one around.

I drove to the clinic and parked in a secluded area of the parking lot. My pulse quickened as I waited for Noah and Liana to return. I had the terrible thought that someone was going to catch me. I was going to be locked in a jail cell the way they'd done to Tristan.

The passenger door opened, and I jumped. My heart settled when I saw it was Noah.

"You got the key?" I asked.

He jingled a key ring in my direction. "They were

sitting on the desk in his office. It was easy to find them and grab them and get out. You?"

I pulled the golden key from my pocket and held it up triumphantly. "A bit *too* easy if you ask me."

I caught sight of Liana making her way across the parking lot. She quickly slid into the back seat. A smile crossed her face when she saw the keys in our hands. "Phase two, complete. Now, we wait until dark."

CHAPTER 17

We returned to Liana's house. I sketched a layout of what I remembered from when I'd been to City Hall, and all the times I'd been there with my dad. All we had to do was get in, grab our magic, and get out.

It was just past midnight when we deemed it safe enough to leave. The three of us dressed in our darkest clothes to minimize the risk of being spotted.

I hadn't wanted Liana to come. It was one thing for Noah and I to get caught. It was another for her. She still had magic they could take away.

"You need me," Liana insisted. She wasn't going to take no for an answer.

We snuck down the hall and into the garage, where I tossed my backpack into the back seat. We'd left the garage door open earlier, and we quietly pulled out of the driveway and onto the street. City Hall was across town, and the streets remained empty as we drove through them.

It took several blocks before I realized I was clenching my fists. If I did have my magic right now, the ocean waves nearby would be going mad. I pulled the vial of ocean water out from under my black shirt and gripped it as we zigzagged through the streets of Sea Haven. Though I knew I couldn't influence the water inside, something about keeping it close to my heart left me with a sense of comfort.

I let the vial fall back under the collar of my shirt. *By the end of the night, I'll be able to control that sea water again.*

The nervous patter of my heart returned when I spotted City Hall ahead of us. Streetlamps brightened the parking lot and the front entrance. Liana turned off the headlights and parked the car in the shadows at the back of the building. She clutched a flashlight in her hands, though we didn't need it right now.

We stayed low as we crossed the grass and ducked behind shrubs.

I surveyed the building and pointed to a spot above the back door. "There's a security camera there."

Noah was so close to me I could feel the heat coming off him. "And one over there."

"I'm on it," Liana said. She'd attached a water bottle to her hip with a carabiner. She unsnapped the top, and water rose at her command. She split the stream of water in two and aimed it at the security cameras. Water swirled around the sensors, which would blur the picture if anyone looked back at the footage.

We made a run for it and stopped at a metal door.

"Ready?" Noah wiggled his eyebrows.

Adrenaline coursed through my system. "Ready."

Noah slipped the silver key inside. Relief flooded through me when I heard the click of the lock disengaging. We were so close!

We entered a dark stairwell lit only by a red emergency light.

"Stay close," Noah whispered.

Apparently, I was too close because in the next step I took, my toes caught his heel.

He shot a glance over his shoulder. "Not that close."

Noah led us down the stairs and through the door at the bottom. We entered a long hallway. The main ceiling lights weren't on, but there were a few dim lights set at the corner between the wall and the ceiling to just barely light the way. We caught sight of a security camera, and Liana used her magic to blur the picture with water again.

I'd never been into the basement of City Hall before Carson Ray led me down here to steal my magic. Looking up and down the hall at all the dark wooden doors, each with their small window in the middle, made it look like an impossible labyrinth. Each door looked the same as the last. I could walk around down here for hours without realizing I'd passed the same door twice.

The hall stretched in both directions, each taking a turn at the end. I knew we needed to head toward the middle of the building.

"This way," I said, nodding to our left.

Before we reached the end of the hall, another hallway cut through to the right. I turned down it. At the end of the hall, it split into two directions again.

"This looks familiar," I whispered.

"Are you sure?" Liana asked. "These halls all look the same."

I nodded, my gaze still fixed on the hall in front of me. I didn't know what it was about the hallway. Maybe it was the spacing of the doors, but I knew I'd been there before. We passed a hall to the right, and I noticed the elevator at the end of it. This was definitely the way they brought me last time. We slowed the closer we came to our target.

I turned to the door I was sure led to the room with the red chair in it. "We're here."

My breathing grew shallow knowing I was this close to my magic. Noah turned to the door.

I glanced toward a room down the hall. This time, the light wasn't on. I wondered if Tristan was still in there, or what the council had done with him.

A shiver ran down my spine. No matter what the

council had done to me, that merman was dangerous. The last thing I wanted was to run into him down here.

"Hurry up," I hissed so quietly I wasn't sure Noah heard me.

The key in his hand twisted in the knob, and the door swung open. My heart leapt. Only one door left. The three of us hurried into the room.

I pulled the golden key from my pocket. Time seemed to slow in the following seconds as I slid the key into the lock. I entered the code I'd seen Dr. Sloan use—2673. My pulse pounded against the sides of my skull, drowning out the sound of the key twisting in the lock.

The door opened. I could hardly breathe; I was so overcome with joy. Rows of glowing vials lined the walls of the room, and I could feel the energy of it all when I stepped inside. Gazing around at the blue hues dancing across the walls, I went speechless in shock. It was all so beautiful, so mesmerizing. When I managed to pull my eyes off the beautiful vials and glance back at Noah, I saw his face showed a similar expression to mine—jaw slack, eyes filled with wonder.

Liana took a cautious step into the room, like she couldn't believe what she was seeing.

"It's amazing, isn't it?" I asked.

"It's incredible," Noah breathed. He seemed awe-struck, like he never expected to see his magic again.

I stepped further into the room, my eyes passing over each vial. One of them in the far-right corner seemed to glow brighter than the rest, its blue much more vibrant. An energy I couldn't pinpoint drew me toward it. The closer I got, the more energized I felt. I reached out toward the vial. Even before my hand clamped around it, I knew. This one was *mine*.

"There are so many," Noah said, startling me so much that I pulled my hand away from the vial. "How do we know which ones are ours?"

I pulled my brows together, looking at him. "Can't you tell?"

I turned back to the bright, blue vial and reached out for it again. I felt so full of life the closer I got. I finally touched it and pulled it off the shelf, holding it close to my chest. Happiness filled my soul. It didn't matter what happened from here on out. All that mattered was that I had my magic back.

Liana held up one of the vials and pointed to the bottom. "They're labeled."

I nearly had to force myself to drag the vial away from my heart to check the label. Sure enough, *Bree Waters* was scrawled across the bottom on a small label.

"Found mine." I held it up with a triumphant smile spread across my face.

"How'd you know that one was yours?" Noah asked.

I clutched the vial tighter—possessively. "It called out to me."

Noah pressed his lips together. "Maybe it's because you haven't been separated from your magic as long as I have."

"You think you lost touch with yours?" I tried my best

to remain focused on the conversation, but it was difficult when the pulsing energy in my hands called my attention.

"Oh." Noah let out a light sound that I couldn't exactly place. Then I noticed his eyes had locked on one of the vials next to me.

"I think you found yours." I smiled and stepped aside so he could finally reunite with the lost piece of himself.

His eyes didn't stray from the vial in front of him. When he pulled the vial off the shelf, he drew it to his chest the same way I had and then breathed a sigh of relief.

"It's wonderful, isn't it?" I asked, still holding my core as close to me as I could. "It makes you feel... so alive... so complete."

Noah didn't turn to me when he spoke, but his voice cracked. "I forgot what it felt like."

When our eyes met again, I knew we were thinking the same thing. "On three?" I asked.

Noah nodded.

"One..." I said.

"Two..." Noah continued.

"Three..." We finished together.

In the same moment, we popped open our vials. The blue glow escaped in a stream as if it were water that wasn't affected by gravity. My magic danced in waves and swirled out of the vial until it wrapped itself around me. It left me feeling warm, comforted. It was like I didn't know who I was until this moment, until I rediscovered a piece of myself that I'd lost. Reuniting with my magic was like the ocean waves reuniting with the shore—they belonged together, and one could not exist without the other.

The stream of magic touched my heart, filling a hole I never knew was there. And then the glowing died as if my magic was a fluid that had soaked into my body, like we'd become one.

For a moment, I just stood there focusing on the energy coursing through my body again. I'd never been so acutely aware of it before. It was so much stronger than when I'd found the vial and held it. When that happened, I somehow felt more energized and alive. This was amplified, and I suddenly felt like I could take on anything.

Noah wore an expression of amazement. He swallowed hard. "How do you feel?"

I couldn't find the words to answer. How could I possibly describe this feeling? Remembering the vial of sea water around my neck, I quickly grabbed for it, pulling it out from under my shirt. Holding it with the ends of my fingers, I pulled the vial to eye-level and channeled my magic through it. The water swirled at my will and then changed directions inside the container, all without me moving.

A wide smile stretched across my face. "I've never felt more like myself."

"Um... guys?" Liana's voice wavered. We both turned to see the terrified look on her face, and my heart sank. "You're going to want to see this."

Stacks of paper sat on the countertop in front of her.

"What is it?" I asked, stepping closer.

Liana flipped through the pages. "It's some sort of manual."

Noah furrowed his brow as he eyed the pages. "*Instructions for Core Storage.*"

Liana began reading out loud. "*A merfolk's core is the source of their power, and therefore extremely valuable. However, cores exhibit a unique and personal value that cannot be transferred, and as such, it is Blue Wave Energy's policy that a merfolk's core can only be stored and not sold alongside other energy products.* What the hell does that mean? What's Blue Wave Energy?"

My body had turned to ice. "I have no idea, but I'm certain the council does. There has to be a reason the rule exists in the first place. What other energy products are they selling?"

Nobody had an answer. My eyes scanned the room, as if I'd find more answers among the glowing cores. Then my gaze fell upon a stone on the countertop. It was a blue stone attached to a string. Recognition hit, and I realized it was the necklace Tristan had been wearing when I found him. It sat next to a vial that glowed like the others, but curiosity had me reaching out for it. I checked the label, and my stomach dropped.

Tristan Adamaris.

I held up the vial. "They stole the merman's core, too."

"Which makes him helpless," Noah pointed out.

"The council said he was dangerous, but maybe it wasn't for the reasons I thought," I said. "What if he knew something he shouldn't?"

Noah cocked an eyebrow. "Like what Blue Wave Energy is, and what *energy products* exactly they're selling?"

I nodded. "Exactly. Either way, we need to speak with Tristan. Carson Ray is hiding more than just these cores, and I intend to figure out exactly what that is."

CHAPTER 18

I took Tristan's core and clutched the string of his necklace in my hand as we left the room. The hair on the back of my neck stood as we snuck down the hall.

"This is the room I saw him in," I said, stopping in front of it. I tried to peer through the window, but the room was dark. I turned to Liana. "Do you still have that flashlight on you?"

"Yeah." She handed it to me, and I clicked it on.

My stomach plummeted when I shone the light through the window. A small cot had been set up in the corner of the room. A man sat curled up on top of it, shaking. He shielded his eyes when the light hit his face. I couldn't mistake the bruises running up his arms.

Carson Ray had tortured him.

Tristan had the same long hair and same matching beard as the first time I saw him, but everything else about him was different. He didn't appear like the strong man I'd first seen, but more like a child—like all the strength had been beat out of him. The brilliant green tail I remembered had been replaced by a pair of legs. He wore modern clothing, including a simple t-shirt and jeans, as well as a pair of sneakers.

He didn't look like a threat at all. I didn't believe for a second anything the council had said about him.

"Open the door!" I begged Noah. "We have to help him!"

My pulse quickened as Noah slid the key into the lock, until the door opened. I flipped on the light and rushed across the room, kneeling at Tristan's side. In this light, he looked even worse than I first thought. His eyes were black and swollen, and his throat was purple with bruises.

"P—please," he begged. "Don't hurt me."

"We aren't here to hurt you," I told him desperately. "We're here to help."

To prove it, I held up the vial that contained his glowing core, along with his necklace. His blue-green eyes stared at me in disbelief.

"W—why would you do that?" he asked in a shaky tone.

"Because I know what it's like to lose your core," I told him.

Tristan's features softened, and recognition crossed his eyes. "You're the girl who found me."

I nodded. "The council sent me away, but I'm back. We're leaving town, and we're taking you with us."

I held up the vial that contained his core, and relief entered his eyes. I popped off the cork, and the magic flooded into him. Tristan breathed a heavy sigh, and a smile touched his lips. I knew the feeling all too well—like in one single moment, you suddenly became whole again.

"Can you stand?" Noah asked.

Tristan hesitated, then nodded. I shoved his necklace into my pocket, and Noah and I helped Tristan to his feet. He was steady on both legs, but I could tell he was weak.

"Let's get him somewhere safe," I said.

Liana glanced up and down the hall, and when she deemed it safe, she gestured us forward. We snuck through the halls until we reached the elevator, where I pressed the button and waited.

The sound of a door falling shut somewhere down the hall startled us all.

"Hey!" a man called.

I whirled around to find a man at least a head taller than me racing toward us. He wore a uniform with a holster at his hip. He must've been a security guard.

"Run!" Noah cried.

The four of us took off sprinting. We couldn't go back the way we came to the stairwell, and we couldn't wait for the elevator. I was certain there was another set of stairs at the other end of the building, but I wasn't sure which hall it was down.

The muscles in my legs protested, and my lungs began to burn with shallow, frightened breaths. I focused on keeping up with Noah in front of me and less on the man behind me, but I couldn't help but listen to the sound of his footsteps pounding on the concrete floor. It felt that with each step I took, he came one step closer.

At the end of the hall, Noah took a left, our only escape. A door leading to a stairwell stood at the end of the hall.

"Stop, or I'll shoot!" the guy shouted.

Noah tossed open the door. It flung open so hard that the sound of it slamming against the wall echoed down the hall.

Tristan was still weak and looked unsteady on his feet. I grabbed his hand to help guide him through the stairwell in the darkness. His fingers were much warmer than the first time I'd met him. Our footsteps echoed through the stairwell as our feet pounded on the stairs in full sprint. At the top of the stairs, I took a sharp right, following the sound of Noah's feet. Tristan followed, and Liana was right behind us.

Noah ran for a door at the end of the hall. He twisted the knob, but the door didn't budge. From behind us, the stairwell door burst open as the security guard chased us down.

A loud *bang* sounded, making my ears ring. I whirled around to see the security guard aiming a smoking pistol at us, and it looked like he was ready to shoot again.

"In here!" Noah cried.

We quickly ducked into an open office, and Liana slammed the door shut behind us, twisting the lock. My heart hammered as the security guard's footsteps raced closer.

"We're cornered!" I cried.

"Not for long," Noah stated.

A large window sat behind the desk. Noah ran over to it, and when he couldn't find a latch, he grabbed the chair behind the desk and threw it at the window.

Glass shattered, raining down on the carpet. My heart lurched as another gunshot sounded—closer this time. The guard was trying to shoot the lock!

"This way!" Noah barked, ushering us all through the broken window.

Tristan crawled through first, then I went. I had to grab the window frame to steady myself. My hands dug into shards of glass, and I winced as they sliced through my palms. I landed on solid ground a moment later. The night air hit me unexpectedly, and a heavy breeze rushed through my hair. Liana and Noah jumped through the window after me, the same time the office door swung open.

"On the ground!" the guard shouted, lifting his gun at us.

"Hurry!" Liana shouted.

We took off running, and a third gunshot rang through the air. Tristan ducked, but I looped my arm under his and guided him around the side of the building. The sound of blood pulsed in my ears as we sprinted to Liana's car.

Liana jumped into the driver's seat, while Noah took the passenger seat. I threw open the back door and helped Tristan inside, before sliding in beside him.

"Go!" I yelled.

The engine roared to life, and the tires spun as Liana hit the gas.

My pulse didn't begin to slow until we were blocks away and the security guard was long out of sight.

Noah placed his hand over his heart to slow his breathing. "We've got to get out of town. Liana, you can drop us off at my car, and we'll be long gone before sunrise."

"I'm not leaving you," Liana insisted, like Noah was crazy.

"You have family here," Noah said. "If you've got a chance to stay—"

"I don't know if I do," she replied. "The security guard saw me. I can't plead my innocence anymore. Wherever you guys go, I go."

While they spoke, I turned to Tristan to inspect his bruises. "Are you okay?"

Tristan looked toward me, but it was more like he was looking *through* me. His eyes wouldn't focus. A moment later, his features paled, and he slumped against me.

I caught him, my arms wrapping around him. When

my hand touched his opposite shoulder, it came away wet with a sticky liquid. I gazed down at my hand in horror to see it coated in blood.

"Guys!" My voice trembled. "We need to get Tristan help *now*. He's been shot."

CHAPTER 19

Going to the hospital was out of the question, and the closest one outside of Sea Haven was over an hour away.

"I know a place we can crash for the night," Liana said.

She drove out of town and pulled into a private driveway tucked behind rocky terrain and palm trees. In the light of the moon, I could see the ocean ahead of us, just a short walk from the house.

"My grandparents stay here on weekends, but they have a townhouse they live in during the week," Liana explained. "We'll be safe here for the night."

Tristan was out cold. Noah draped one of Tristan's

arms around his neck and hoisted him out of the car, while Liana and I hurried inside. I found a first-aid kit under the sink in the bathroom, and Liana gathered some towels. Blood dripped down Tristan's arm and onto the hardwood.

"In here," Liana told Noah, gesturing him to the bedroom. She pressed a towel firmly to the wound on Tristan's arm and helped Noah lay him on the bed.

I got to work inspecting the wound. I didn't have any medical training, but my mother had taught me first-aid basics. "There's no bullet. It looks like the bullet grazed him. I'm going to clean the wound and bandage it up to stop the bleeding. If it gets any worse or gets infected, we'll have to take him to a hospital."

The blood drained from Liana's face. "We can't take him back to Sea Haven. The council will have us arrested. Any other hospital could be dangerous if they discover his magic. Isn't this what the council warns against? Isn't this why they take your magic when you leave?"

"I don't give a damn what the council says," I sneered. "This man needs help. I'm going to do my best, but if it's not enough, then we need to get him proper medical care."

Liana hesitated, then nodded. "All right."

Liana and Noah left the room while I cleaned Tristan's wound and bandaged it as tightly as I could. The bleeding had slowed, but I worried about the blood he'd already lost. I cleaned up, then left Tristan alone to sleep.

I found Liana preparing food in the kitchen. "Where's Noah?"

She gestured toward the back door. "He went down to the beach."

I entered the sunroom off the back of the house and set the first-aid kit on the table there. I looked out the windows to see Noah's silhouette standing on the beach. The distant sound of ocean waves seemed to whisper in my ears, calling out to me and begging me to reunite with them once more.

I opened the door and inhaled a long breath, then took my first step toward the ocean. When my bare feet hit sand, a wave of peace washed over me. The sand felt so serene, like for a moment I could forget everything that happened.

Noah turned to me when he heard me approach. "How's Tristan doing?"

"I think he'll be all right." I stopped when my toes hit the water. The chilly waves felt amazing on my feet. I bent to scoop up a small amount of water. Droplets swirled in my hands, filling me with a sense of pride.

"The water's tempting, isn't it?" Noah asked with a knowing smile.

"It's amazing. I feel *really* powerful." I let the droplets fall from my hands and back into the waves, then I lifted my palms. A huge wave at least thirty feet high swelled above us. It was one of the largest waves I'd ever made, and I still felt like I could keep going. I didn't want to overexert myself, though, so I ordered the wave to settle back into the sea calmly.

Noah's eyebrows shot up. "Impressive."

That was all he said as his gaze locked on the horizon. I didn't have to see into his eyes to know what kind of look had settled over them. His silence said it all. Noah was soaking it all in, enjoying finally being home. He remained quiet for so long that I thought he could have stayed like that forever, but finally, he spoke.

"I don't know why I ever left," he admitted, turning his gaze toward me.

"You didn't have a choice."

Noah shoved his hands into his pockets. "I did, though. Even if it wasn't the choice they gave me, I could've run away and taken my magic with me—just like you're doing. At the time, I just wanted to go. I didn't realize what I was giving up."

"How could you ever *want* to leave?" I wondered.

He pursed his lips like he wasn't sure he should tell me his story. Then, like he decided he could trust me, he sighed. "I lost my parents. My dad died in a construction accident two years ago; my mom from a stroke not long before I left. I'm an only child, so I didn't have any family left. My grandparents are long gone. So there I was, with this option to pay for my crimes, or get out and see more of the world. I was living with this constant memory of my parents, and I thought that if I could get away from Sea Haven, I'd be able to get over it. Turns out you never get over something like that."

I couldn't even pretend to know what he'd gone through. "Noah, I'm sorry. I shouldn't have gotten you involved—"

"Don't apologize," he said quickly. "I'm glad you did."

His gaze turned down to the sand. "This past year, I haven't felt myself. I thought it was grief, and it was, but I didn't realize it was more than that. I wasn't just grieving my parents. There was a piece of me missing, too, and I didn't realize it until I got it back."

"Nobody, not even the Sea Haven Council, should have the right to take something like this away from us," I stated firmly.

Noah nodded. "My core is familiar, but different, too. It's like I need to learn who I am all over again."

"I'm going to be here to help you figure it out," I promised.

Noah swallowed deeply and bent to scoop up a handful of water. He stared at it intensely for several long seconds until it began to swirl in his hands. I eyed him curiously as he focused on the water. Slowly, it began to form an upwards funnel, defying gravity as he manipulated it. The funnel widened at the top to form into the shape of a rose. Noah held his creation in my direction.

I reached out to take it from him, but when our fingers touched, my focus crumbled, and the rose melted in our hands, dripping off them into the shallow water beneath us.

"Hey." Noah smirked playfully. "I worked hard on that."

I chucked. "It was beautiful."

"Thanks, Bree. I'll get the hang of all this again."

I shot him a shy smile. It was strange hearing my name

roll off his tongue. I was surprised to find it somewhat satisfying. "It looks like you remember it pretty well."

The sound of the waves lapping against the shore filled the momentary silence.

"Noah, can I ask you something?"

"Anything," he replied softly.

"Why'd you agree to come with me?"

He didn't answer right away, and for a moment I thought he wouldn't. Then he spoke softly. "You reminded me of home."

I expected him to leave it at that, but he continued. "It's different out there. The people aren't quite the same as they are here. I had a hard time fitting in."

"And *I* have a hard time believing that," I replied. "I always thought you were the type of guy who could fit in anywhere."

Noah scoffed. "When I saw you on my doorstep, it was... familiar. I know we've only ever talked a few times before, but I knew that of all the people in that city, you'd understand me best."

"And yet I still don't know very much about you."

Noah stared out at the open water. "What do you want to know?"

I shrugged. "Tell me a secret."

Noah pressed his lips together. "How about you tell me one first?"

"I already told you a bunch—the fish in the pool, the toilet papering. Those are my secrets."

"You must have more than that."

"By my count, you have to tell me at least two before I spill another."

The corners of his lips twitched. "Those weren't exactly secrets, though. Everyone knew you were involved. You kind of have a reputation for mischief."

I held my chin high. "I'll have you know that I managed a solid B average in high school and never once ended up in detention."

Noah chuckled and shook his head. "All right, you want to know a secret? I... used to have the biggest crush on you in middle school."

My breath caught. I knew I had to say something back, but I couldn't find the words. "I—what—why...?"

Noah shrugged with a smile I could tell he was trying to hide. "I was thirteen. You were cute."

"I'm flattered?" The words came out sounding like a question.

"I remember this one time I was at my locker and you were walking down the hall with your friends and laughing. You made some sort of witty comment. I don't remember what it was anymore. I just remember thinking that you looked so confident and that I might really enjoy your company." He shrugged like it didn't matter, but he still wouldn't look at me.

"You should have said something," I told him softly.

"Eh, it was just a little crush," he said like it didn't matter.

It mattered to me. I never imagined someone would have liked me back then. Noah was another story. I would've considered going out with him if he'd said anything.

"Your turn," Noah said, pulling me from my thoughts. The blush had left his face for the most part, but I could still see the embarrassment written in the smile he was trying to hide.

"I don't really have any secrets."

"Right," he said sarcastically with a nod.

I sucked a breath between my teeth. "I might have one, but you're not going to like it."

"Try me," he challenged.

"When we were in middle school, I was the one who tied your shoes together during the first day of school assembly."

Noah's jaw dropped. "You're kidding."

I shook my head and pressed my lips together. "I was late getting into the gym because I was in the bathroom. You were sitting on the end of the bleachers, and I noticed your shoes were untied. I snuck under the bleachers and tied them together. I feel really bad about it now."

"You should. I chipped a tooth because of you."

My hand shot over my mouth. "Are you serious?"

A lopsided smile that sent my heart flipping in my chest stretched across Noah's face. "No."

"You jerk!" I shoved him playfully.

He nudged me back, and my heart fluttered. "I think I'm going to have to retract what I said before. You don't deserve the crush I had on you."

"You can't just take that back! It's fact. You liked me."

He smiled. "I shouldn't have, now that I know you were the one who sent me falling down the bleachers on my first day of eighth grade."

I laughed. "It's still one of the funniest things I've ever seen. Those were some good times."

Noah's smile faded. "Yeah. It's hard to leave it all behind."

My gaze dropped to the wave lapping at my feet. "I wish we didn't have to."

"Hey." Noah's voice had turned serious. "It's all going to be all right. You know that, don't you?"

I didn't—not really. I had no idea what was going to happen.

When I didn't respond, Noah reached for my hand. He touched the cut I'd gotten when I crawled through the window, and I winced.

He immediately drew away. "Are you okay?"

"I cut my hand on the window."

"Let me look," he offered.

My pulse quickened as he took my hand in his. I couldn't take my eyes off him as he studied my palm.

He wore a deep, caring expression, but he couldn't see much in the dark. "We should go back to the house."

He led me across the sand and back up the hill. We entered the sunroom, and he turned on the light and sat me down at the table. He took my hand in his and closely inspected the cut. His warm breath brushed across my skin, making my heart skip a beat.

"It's not too bad—" I started to say, but he moved my hand, and I gasped.

"I think I see a shard of glass. Hold on." Noah opened the first-aid kit and pulled out a pair of tweezers. His fingers gently moved over mine, and all I could do was sit as still as possible, hoping he didn't notice the quickening of my pulse.

Noah pinched something in my palm, then drew a tiny shard of glass from my skin. Blood sprang from a small cut, and he quickly wrapped it in bandages.

"There," he said proudly. "How does that feel?"

I flexed my hand, and the sharp ache that had been there before was gone. "Much better. Thank you."

A slight smile touched his lips. "Glad I could help."

The door to the sunroom burst open then, and Liana rushed inside. The urgency in her features made my stomach plummet. "Tristan is up."

CHAPTER 20

We hurried into the bedroom. Tristan groaned as he tried to sit upright.

"You should lay down," I insisted. "You lost a lot of blood."

Tristan looked around in confusion, and his eyes fell on the bandage around his bicep. He studied it for a moment, before his gaze turned toward me. The warmth in his blue-green eyes made my pulse quicken. "Thank you for rescuing me."

The expression on his face told me he was truly thankful, but it was more than that. It was like he wasn't just thanking me for tonight but that he was thanking me for more—for the night I found him on the beach, perhaps.

I sat in the chair next to the bed. "What did they do to you?"

Tristan leaned his back against the pillow. "I came here seeking help, and I was treated like a criminal."

"Help?" I asked.

"My pod is in danger," Tristan told us. "Not far from our city, a company has begun underwater mining. It's polluting our waters and killing off our resources. We thought your people could help us—to negotiate with the humans and cease their mining operation, without revealing our existence."

"We didn't know your people existed," I remarked. "Not until you washed up on our beach."

Tristan winced as he resituated himself on the bed. "We have remained hidden for centuries, in order to protect ourselves. We came here to form an alliance."

"We?" Noah asked.

Something dark flashed behind Tristan's eyes. "I came here with five other men. When we got close to shore, something changed—like something was fighting against our magic. Our magic caused a storm we couldn't control, and the others were lost."

Sheer heartbreak filled the room. He was delicate with his words, but the implications were clear—his friends had died in that storm.

"Your councilmembers took me to their headquarters and questioned me," Tristan said. "If I'd have known the hostile environment we were swimming into, we never would have come."

"Sea Haven is supposed to be a peaceful place," I told him. "What they did to you isn't normal. It isn't right."

"What do you know about this company that's mining your resources?" Noah asked. "Does it have anything to do with Blue Wave Energy?"

Tristan shook his head. "The company that threatens our ocean is called Ocean Rock. They haven't discovered us yet, but it's only a matter of time. They're killing off our fish—our people are barely surviving."

"How many people?" Liana asked.

"Ten thousand," Tristan replied. "The Luna pod isn't much smaller than the Sea Haven pod. Apart from your people, we're all that's left."

My jaw hung slack. "How's that possible? We thought merfolk had died centuries ago—that our magic was all that was left of them. But our magic is limited. We can't even grow tails."

Tristan eyed me curiously. "How do the stories go here in Sea Haven?"

I knew this story by heart. My dad used to tell it to me every night as a bedtime story. *Everyone* in Sea Haven knew this one.

"When the gods created the world, it was divided into land and sea," I started. "Humans were created to rule the land, and merfolk were given the powers to control the sea. Our fins could become legs on land, so that we could ally with the humans and work together to keep our planet safe. The gods had designed us to work together."

I breathed a heavy sigh. "But fights broke out, and the alliances fell. Merfolk descended into the deep ocean, but humans brought their boats, hunting the merfolk and chasing them away from their resources. Mermaids lured sailors with their siren call and killed them to keep their pods safe. But the further they were driven out to sea, the fewer resources they had. Merfolk were dying off, and their numbers dwindled, until there was one pod left."

Tristan nodded, like he knew the story so far.

"Then, over two-hundred years ago, a young mermaid named Seraphina fell in love with a human sailor named Truan," I continued. "He brought her to land. They were from two different worlds, but they had a baby together. A war erupted over the child, and the two of them ran away. Seraphina's family blamed Truan's for her disappearance while Truan's people blamed Seraphina's. Truan's family went after the merfolk, and the pod broke in two—those who stayed on land to blend in with the humans to protect themselves, and those who remained at sea. Truan's family hunted the last of the sea pod to extinction. We are what remains of the land pod's descendants. With each generation that we bred with humans, our magic dwindled, until our ancestors closed off the town. People weren't allowed in or out, because if we continued breeding with humans, we would eventually lose all our magic."

Tristan shook his head. "That's where our stories diverge. The sea pod wasn't hunted to extinction. Legend says Truan's family discovered a powerful weapon, and our pod ran. They went into hiding for their own safety."

"We thought your pod had died. Our council didn't know you survived. That's why they tortured you for information," I said.

Tristan nodded. "Yes. The last we heard of your people, your magic was strong, but we haven't made contact in centuries. We had no idea of what had become of your pod."

"You keep calling us a pod," Liana said. "We don't call ourselves that. Our magic has been so diluted, we're hardly merfolk anymore."

"Tristan's stronger than us. The council must've wanted something from him," I remarked.

Noah crossed his arms. "Perhaps they want that weapon he mentioned."

"I don't know what the weapon was, or where to find it," Tristan said. "*We* were the ones driven into hiding. If we had a weapon, why would we run?"

"If that's the case, what did the council want from you?" Liana asked.

"They asked me questions about my people—about our magic and our knowledge," Tristan said. "Apart from my pod's existence, I don't think I told them anything they didn't already know. We have trained professionals who travel ashore—explorers, if you will. They gather knowledge about the modern world and bring that back to our people. Your people already have all the knowledge we have."

"What did they learn about your magic?" I wondered.

"I can do anything any merfolk can—control storms, manipulate water, talk to fish, and breathe underwater indefinitely. I can compel with a siren song, and I have a supersonic scream," Tristan explained.

I furrowed my brow. "That's everything our stories tell us about our ancestors. They must've taken your core so you couldn't use your magic against them."

"They took my core to compel me," Tristan said.

I tilted my head. "You mean so you wouldn't compel them?"

Tristan shook his head. "Merfolk cannot compel other merfolk. But once they took my core, they could compel me to answer any questions they wanted. When I didn't answer to their satisfaction, they tortured me. It's like they expected me to know things I didn't."

"That's not possible," I insisted. "We don't have the power to compel."

Tristan's eyebrows shot up. "The head of your council does."

I reeled back in my chair. "If Carson Ray can compel, that means he has full merfolk abilities."

The room went dead silent as we all took this in. It seemed impossible.

"Could Carson be from the Luna pod?" Noah asked.

"I don't know," I admitted. "He's been in Sea Haven forever. His father was the council head before him, and *his* father before that. It's possible his mother isn't from here, unless..."

I gasped. "The weapon Tristan mentioned. What if it's the stone Dr. Sloan used to take our cores, but on a bigger scale? If the stone can take our cores, then it's strong enough to siphon our magic in pieces."

"Blue Wave Energy..." Liana whispered. "They're selling energy products, and our magic definitely fits the bill."

"If the weapon is strong enough to affect everyone in Sea Haven all at once, then Carson must have some way to counteract it so he isn't affected like the rest of us," I said. "That's how he could compel Tristan once he took his core."

I got lightheaded thinking about it. If we were right, this changed everything we knew about our people.

"This is... insane," Liana breathed. "The council can't really be *stealing* our magic."

"But they can," Noah stated. "And they've made sure that nobody with magic can leave."

Nausea slammed into my gut, and I wanted to hurl. "That's why they took our core before we left—not because it's dangerous for us, but because it's dangerous for *them*. If we got too far away from Sea Haven, they wouldn't be able to control our magic, and we'd know what they were doing."

My whole body shook. "I used to think Sea Haven was this perfect place, but is it worth the price we have to pay? We could have far more magic than we ever realized, and Carson's just *taking* it. If our people knew what he was doing, they'd never stand for this. We have to stop him!"

Noah held his hands up. "Slow down, Bree. What are we going to do? Raid Carson's house? We haven't slept or eaten anything, and Tristan has a *bullet wound*. Even if we could physically take Carson on, we don't know how this magic works or what we're up against."

My shoulders sagged. Noah was right, but I wasn't about to walk away from Sea Haven—not after tonight.

"We'll get some rest," I agreed. "But then we're getting answers. Whatever Carson Ray and Blue Wave Energy is up to, we're going to figure it out—and we're going to expose them."

"Everyone should get some food, then head to bed," Liana suggested. "I made soup. My grandparents have three room. Tristan can stay in here, and Bree and I can share a room. I'll show Noah to the third guest room."

Liana gestured to Noah, and I started following behind them until I remembered something. I turned back to Tristan and dug into my pocket.

"I almost forgot. This is yours." I held up his necklace.

A hint of a smile touched Tristan's lips. He took the necklace and ran his fingers over the stone, admiring it. "Aquamarine—the stone of my people. Your council took it from me when they locked me in that room. I thought I'd lost it forever."

Tristan tied the string around his neck and tucked the stone under his shirt.

"Nothing Carson Ray does will last forever," I told him. "I'll make sure of that."

CHAPTER 21

It was a restless sleep. To think that Carson Ray was using a centuries-old weapon against his own people was unbelievable...

And yet I believed it to my core.

I woke the next morning to the sound of raindrops pattering against the window. I knew I wasn't going to get back to sleep, so I rolled out of bed and dug in my backpack for my toothbrush. I went to the bathroom without changing out of my pajamas—a pair of spandex shorts with an oversized t-shirt over a sports bra.

I let the water in the sink run longer than it needed to, enjoying the way my magic pulsed at the connection.

Having my magic back was like being able to breathe after days spent gasping for air.

A scream tore through the house, startling me. I didn't think—I just ran. I sprinted down the hall toward the sound of Liana's cry, my pulse pounding. My heart stalled when I skidded to a halt in the bedroom doorway.

A man dressed in black had dragged Liana out of bed and held a gun to the side of her head. His hands were tangled in her hair, and she was on her knees. Tears beaded in her eyes as she gazed up at me in horror.

"Leave her alone—!" I started, but my words halted as something hard pressed into my back.

"Walk," a voice sneered from behind me.

Slowly, I lifted my hands in surrender. The last thing I wanted was for them to hurt one of my friends. I followed the man's orders and walked down the hall. I tried to remain calm and take in every detail I could, but my mind raced a million miles per hour.

The man led me into the kitchen. Noah and Tristan were already there on their knees, guns pointed to the side of their heads. In the middle of it all was Carson Ray.

Carson appeared nonchalant, like this was any ordinary morning. He wore a dark suit and red tie and folded his hands neatly in front of himself.

My teeth gritted as the man behind me forced me to my knees beside Noah, though I never took my gaze off Carson. Liana whimpered as one of the men shoved her to the ground beside me. They pulled our arms behind our backs and fitted handcuffs onto our wrists. Five men surrounded us, and there was nowhere to run without it ending with a bullet to the back.

"So you found us," I stated coolly. "What are you going to do with us now?"

Carson's expression gave nothing away. He crossed his hands in front of himself calmly. "I tried to be reasonable—tried to be *understanding*—but you had to stick your nose where it didn't belong."

"You *stole* my core!" I shouted. The man behind me shoved the gun deeper into my back.

I couldn't help but notice Carson had completely ignored my question.

Noah didn't seem frightened by the guns, and he narrowed his gaze at Carson. "What else are you *stealing*?"

Carson gave a chilling laugh. "I'm sure by now you have your suspicions."

"How are you pulling it off?" I demanded. "You've got to have more power than that little stone Dr. Sloan used on us."

Carson narrowed his eye at me. "Trust me, you don't know what you're dealing with."

"We know you have the power to steal people's cores," I accused. "What's to keep you from stealing other pieces of their magic?"

"I am *helping* our people," Carson snapped. "Do you really think the town makes all its money off *fishing*? Our people require resources, and that involves an exchange."

"Without their consent," I sneered. "That's why you take our magic before we leave town—so you can keep up the charade and no one knows what they're capable of."

Carson cocked an eyebrow. "Our people wouldn't know how to use their magic if they had it. Merfolk tails would send them swimming off to sea—they'd be discovered. Siren compulsion would put our people in jeopardy."

Noah's breaths grew shallow beside me. "We've had full merfolk abilities all along, haven't we? Why let us keep any magic at all?"

"A merfolk's core cannot be converted into energy, but the magic itself that it creates? That is a *very* powerful resource." Greed flashed in Carson's eyes. "We provide the town just enough magic to satisfy their call to the water. Every time a merfolk uses their magic, we can harness more of it, convert it into energy, and sell it as fuel. That money goes back into our community."

"What does money matter?" I growled. "Our people are connected by *magic*, not money."

Carson scoffed. "You've never known the full extent of your magic. You can't miss something you've never had. My family has been harnessing merfolk magic for centuries, and no one has complained until you came along. No one who had anything to say about it, at least."

His meaning was clear. He'd compelled them to stay quiet.

It was in that moment that I realized he had compelled *me*. After Carson took my core, he warned me to never tell a human soul what had happened, but he'd messed up. None of us were human—we were merfolk.

I was almost certain he'd done the same to Noah, and I realized then that Noah hadn't explicitly *told* me the council had taken his magic. He'd only ever confirmed what I'd already guessed. Now that we had our cores back, Carson's compulsion didn't work on us.

"I'm sure the town would have something to say about it if they knew," I stated coolly.

Carson smirked. "And that's why they never will."

"So why don't you kill us already?" I questioned.

Carson's smirk grew wider, like he was amused. "I don't have to kill you when I can simply compel you. Dr. Sloan is preparing the sea stone now."

So the weapon had a name—*sea stone*.

"You will come with us and give up your core," Carson said. "Once you've given up your magic for good, you will forget this ever happened."

"My people will come looking for me," Tristan declared.

"And we will be ready for them if they do." Carson turned back to me. "As for you, you will leave Sea Haven and never return."

He spoke as if we would go through with this willingly, like we'd be *okay* with him using his siren call against us. If he took our cores, he could compel us to do anything—even forget.

"I will *never* let you take my core again," I sneered.

Carson laughed, and the blood in my veins turned to ice. "I think you'll find that you will, Miss Waters."

Carson snapped his fingers, and footsteps sounded

down the hall. Another man stepped into the kitchen, and I realized I recognized him. It was Jarod Erickson, the man who had driven me to the airport—and he dragged a helpless man in handcuffs behind him.

Jarod shoved the man to the ground and pointed a gun at his face. The world seemed to shift on its axis as my stomach dropped out of my abdomen.

I barely managed to speak past the terror rising in my throat. "Dad?"

CHAPTER 22

Tears brimmed in my father's eyes. "Bree, I'm so sorry."

"It's not your fault, Dad," I insisted desperately, before turning my rage on Carson. "Let him go! All he ever did was follow *your* orders. He did nothing wrong!"

Carson smirked. "I didn't bring your father here to punish him, Miss Waters."

Jarod grabbed my father by the collar and shoved his gun into the side of his head. The implication was clear. Carson had brought my father to punish *me*.

"On your feet," the man behind me growled, pressing the barrel of his gun hard into my back.

I had no choice but to stand and force my shaking feet to move under me as the men marched us out of the house. A large black van was parked outside behind a big SUV. The councilmembers shoved the five of us into the back of the van and slammed the doors. There were no seats, so we were forced to sit on the floor.

Jarod slid into the drivers' seat, while another councilmember sat in the passenger seat. The others got into the SUV, and the vehicles roared to life.

My father ducked his head. "Bree, I can't tell you how sorry I am. I had no idea any of this was going on. I never would've let them send you away—"

"Quiet back there!" Jarod yelled.

We all went silent, but I swore my pounding heart could be heard from a mile away. I peered between the front seats, keeping my eyes out the window. The wipers swished quickly, and I couldn't see much, but I could tell we were headed back into town.

I was certain they were taking us back to City Hall, where they would strip us of our cores once again. Carson said he didn't intend to kill us, but I knew he wouldn't hesitate to order his men to pull the trigger if we didn't do exactly as he said.

We followed the SUV into town. We were only a few blocks from City Hall when Dad lowered his voice. "On my signal, get ready to run."

I shot him a questioning look, "Dad, what are you—?"

"Hey!" the councilmember in the front seat shouted. At first, I thought he was yelling at me, until I turned my gaze forward. The SUV in front of us had turned down another street, and Jarod was turning in the opposite direction. "Where are you going?"

Jarod didn't answer. Instead, he snatched the man's gun out of his hand, then rammed his elbow up into his face. The van jerked to the side, tires squealing. I was thrown into Noah, who caught me. The councilmember in the passenger seat sagged forward. He'd been knocked out cold.

I barely had a moment to process it all before Jarod slammed on the breaks. My father maneuvered his bound hands to grab the door handle, then shoved the back door open with his shoulder the same time Jarod jumped out of the vehicle.

"Quickly!" Jarod cried. He came up behind my father, and something clicked. My father's wrists broke free, and the handcuffs fell to the pavement.

Jarod was helping us escape! My father must've planned this with him.

The rest of us jumped out of the vehicle. The rain had picked up now, and we were soaked within moments.

Jarod quickly undid my cuffs. "I am deeply sorry for the part I played in this, Bree."

I looked up at him, and it became clear to me then that Jarod didn't understand what the council was doing when he drove me to the airport, and now he wanted to help us escape to make up for it.

"This way!" my father called, gesturing us to follow.

We hurried around the side of the van, and I finally realized where we were. A long dock stretched out in front of us, lined with all kinds of boats. Jarod had brought us to the marina.

My legs moved under me as my feet pounded on the dock, but my feet were faster than my brain. We were nearly to the end of the marina before I could really think about what was happening.

"Take my boat!" Jarod ushered us onto a small sailboat.

Tristan and Noah jumped in. Noah reached out to take my hand, and Tristan helped Liana onto the boat. My pulse roared in my ears. I turned, expecting my father to climb onto the boat behind us, but he remained on the dock with Jarod. They scrambled to untie the ropes anchoring the sailboat to the dock. My father tossed the ropes back onto the boat as we started drifting away.

"Go!" Dad cried. "Get as far away as possible."

Tires squealed in the distance, and my stomach lurched, as if I'd been punched in the gut. A large SUV came to a stop at the end of the marina, and Carson Ray jumped out of the vehicle.

"Dad! You have to come with us!" I cried.

"Jarod and I will hold them off!" Dad yelled back. "You have to leave now! I love you, Bree."

Dad lifted his palms, and a wave rushed up to carry us far away from the marina.

"Dad!" I screamed. Water streamed down my face, but I couldn't tell what was tears and what was rain. I ran to the back of the boat, like somehow I could reach out to my father, but he was at least fifty yards away now.

Noah ran after me and grabbed me around the waist. My father had already turned his attention to the councilmembers running toward him.

"Bree, your dad gave us a chance to escape," Noah insisted. "We have to go."

The waves carried us further, but I couldn't take my eyes off the dock. My father and Jarod worked together to create a huge wave that crashed over the councilmembers. Several of them were swept up in the wave and knocked off the dock, but Carson Ray didn't miss a beat in his step. He narrowed his gaze on me. Carson yanked his tie off, then tossed his suit coat into the water.

My father aimed another massive wave at him, but Carson threw his hands outward, and the wave stopped dead, hovering in mid-air. Carson took control of the wave and flicked his wrist. The water smashed down on my father and Jarod.

"No!" I screamed.

The water splashed off the dock, and when the wave receded, my father and Jarod were nowhere in sight. All I saw was Carson, rolling up his sleeves as he marched down the dock in pursuit of us. He reached the end of the marina and dove into the water.

"We have to move faster!" Noah cried. "Let's get these sails up!"

Noah went to untie the sails, while Tristan lifted his hands and formed a huge wave that carried us further out to sea. I couldn't bring myself to move. My hands tightened around the metal railing surrounding the boat as I stared toward the marina. I caught sight of my father and Jarod climbing back onto the dock, but Carson had disappeared into the water. He couldn't be fast enough to reach us. Tristan's wave had carried us so far out to sea that the marina was a mere dot on the horizon now.

The storm picked up around us. Rain pounded down harder, and waves rocked the boat from side to side.

"Tristan!" Liana cried as she held on to the railing for dear life. "Your waves are out of control!"

"I'm trying to control them!" Tristan panicked. "Something's fighting against me."

A shadowy figure darted through the water, and my heart lurched.

"There's something below us!" I shouted.

I barely got the words out before a massive column of water spiraled upward, like an ominous tornado rising high above our boat. The sprout carried the shadowy figure above the surface of the sea, until the creature emerged from the water. I realized in horror that it was Carson Ray, but he looked different than I'd ever seen him before.

Carson wore his white button-down shirt, but the bottom half of him where his trousers should be shimmered with red scales.

Carson Ray had a tail.

CHAPTER 23

"I will not let you get away and breathe our secrets to another soul!" Carson yelled over the roar of the wind. "You love your precious sea so much, but you haven't seen what it can do at my command. The ocean will claim you, and you will be lost to sea like so many merfolk before you."

Carson thrust his hand outward, and a wave crashed into the side of the boat with a force that knocked the four of us off our feet. Tristan fell overboard, but Noah, Liana, and I held on to the railing tightly. The boat swayed in the other direction violently, forcing our heads under water. I inhaled a sharp breath of salt water, and though I could breathe under water, the cold of the ocean shocked me.

The boat bobbed upright again, and Carson's laughter echoed through the air. It was obvious he was only getting started.

"You will not touch them," Tristan's voice called over the storm.

A second water sprout rose upward, until Tristan was eye-to-eye with Carson Ray. Tristan's long green tail appeared, the ends of it flicking like he was poised for an attack.

Carson laughed. "You may have access to your precious magic, but you do not know these waters as I do."

"I was born in the sea!" Tristan raged. "I know it well, and I will not let you use it to hurt these people."

Carson lifted his hands. "Then by all means, show me what the Luna pod can do!"

Wind whipped by us, and the waves swelled to epic proportions. I couldn't see anything beyond the fifty-foot waves growing around us. Tristan flicked his tail and dove for Carson the same moment Carson aimed a huge wave straight at our boat.

Liana's screams tore through the air, and my stomach flipped as the boat capsized. The side of my head slammed into something hard, and I was swept up in a strong current. My feet toppled over my head, and I lost my bearings as I tumbled through the water.

Terror rocked my body when I finally slowed and looked around. I couldn't see a thing through the darkness.

I inhaled a heavy gulp of salt water, but it didn't calm my nerves. I had no idea which way to swim to the surface. Water surrounded me on all sides so that even with my magic, I couldn't sense the sandy ocean bed, nor the break in the surface of the water. I'd never been in waters so deep before.

Hands landed on me, and I instinctually shoved them away. I intended to use my magic to propel me far away from the assailant, but his hand gripped me tighter. He wrapped his arms around me, pulling my head to his chest. I could hear his heartbeat, and I felt his legs brush against mine.

My pulse settled as I drew away and my eyes adjusted to the darkness. I could just barely make out Noah's features. He pointed upward toward the surface, and I followed him.

We broke the surface of the water, but the storm was stronger than ever. Waves crashed over our heads, pushing us downward again. I swam upward and gasped a breath.

"Where's Liana?" I shouted.

"I didn't see her!" Noah yelled back.

Rain poured down on us, and lightning cracked overhead. Through the downpour, I could make out waterspouts rising from the ocean, spinning like whips toward shadows in the water. A stream of water hit Tristan square in the chest, sending him spinning through the air.

I caught sight of a red tail in the distance. "Noah!" I shouted, pointing. "I see Carson. We have to help Tristan!"

Noah and I ducked our heads under the surface again,

and we used our magic to propel ourselves toward our enemy. A heavy wave pounded down above us, and I spotted a flash of red. Then came a shimmering green as Tristan dove to attack Carson. A stream of water erupted from Tristan's palm, pounding into Carson's chest and forcing him to sink toward the bottom of the ocean.

Carson sank deeper and deeper... until he opened his mouth, and a blast of energy sent Tristan's stream of water hurtling back in his direction. Water expanded out at all angles, and the muffled sound of a sonic scream filled my ears. The soundwaves hit us, making my body shake to the bones as we went tumbling backward.

Noah reached out for me, and I caught his fingers in mine. I ordered the water to slow us down, until we righted ourselves. Raging waters swirled around us, and I glanced around frantically for the sight of Tristan's green tail, but I didn't see it.

Where's Tristan!? I tried to shout, but no sound came out.

Noah and I used our powers to propel us toward the surface. The waves were huge now, creating gigantic mountains and valleys out of water. I steadied myself on the surface, but it took everything I had in me not to get caught up in the waves. Overhead, the skies were as dark as night, with nothing to light our way but the flash of lightning.

"I can't see them!" I shouted to Noah.

He didn't get a chance to respond before we were swept up in a whirlwind and tossed into the air. I ordered the raindrops to come together and catch me. Off in the distance, I spotted Carson and Tristan at the surface.

Tristan swirled his hand through the air, commanding a column of water to spiral upward and carry Carson high into the sky. Then the column exploded outward, sending water raining down in all directions. Carson fell from at least a hundred feet up. Tristan kept his focus on the water below, fighting to keep Carson from taking control of the wave. Carson hit the water *hard*, then disappeared below the surface.

I held my breath, but I didn't see him anywhere. Then came a splash behind Tristan.

Carson sprang up from the ocean below and locked his arm around Tristan's throat. He used his other hand to rip the bandage off Tristan's arm. He rammed his thumb into Tristan's skin, tearing open the wound. Tristan screamed as blood spurted from the open cut.

Tristan spun around and smacked his tail hard against the side of Carson's head. Carson lost his grip, but almost immediately, he manipulated the water to call up seaweed from the ocean floor. The seaweed curled around Tristan's throat at Carson's command.

Whether above the surface or below, Tristan still needed to breathe. If Carson held on much longer, he'd strangle him.

I thrust my hands outward, and a wave rushed in Carson's direction. The same time, Noah formed a column of water. Our magic collided when it reached Carson, crashing down on him from various angles.

Carson merely shook his head, like it was nothing more than a splash. We weren't strong enough to create waves that would rival his in this storm. I tried swimming closer, but the waves only pulled me back.

"Bree!" I heard Liana call my name, and I turned to see her waving to us. The dorsal fins of three dolphins stuck out of the water beside her. "We have to get closer!"

Liana grabbed on to one of the dolphins, and they swam over to us. My magic connected with their energy, and realized that one in particular was familiar.

"Delphina?" I asked in disbelief.

Delphina threw her head back. I'd considered this dolphin a friend—she had brought me shells, and I gave her fish—but I never expected her to put herself in danger for me.

A calmness washed through me. Delphina was telling me not to worry, that she wasn't afraid.

"We have to work together." I curled my legs around Delphina's back, while Noah took the other dolphin. "If we combine our magic, we might be able to create a wave big enough to stop him!"

The dolphins leapt into the air, then dove under water. They swam faster than they'd ever taken me, until they broke the surface not far from Carson.

"Now!" I yelled.

My friends and I lifted our hands, and we used our magic to pull the momentum of one of the massive waves over Carson's head. The wave crested over top of him, and

Carson caught sight of us on the backs of our dolphins a moment before he was pushed under.

The seaweed around Tristan's neck loosened, and he yanked it off himself. Our dolphins quickly swam over to him. Tristan gasped as he draped his arm over the neck of my dolphin.

"He's strong, I'll give him that," Tristan said.

"He shouldn't be able to defeat us all together," I insisted. "There has to be a reason he can access powers as strong as yours. He's been taking ours from us; there must be a way to get it back. If we can all access our full merfolk abilities, then he doesn't stand a chance—"

I cut off as bubbles from under the water tickled my legs. The water around us grew more violent, and I clutched tighter to my dolphin's dorsal fin.

"What's happening?" Liana cried.

A wave swelled up around us, towering so tall I couldn't see the top of it. High above us, the surface of the water broke, and Carson laughter echoed louder than the thunder. He rode on the back of two terrifying beasts larger than our dolphins. The creatures bared their endless rows of razor-sharp teeth.

Carson had returned, and he'd brought two sharks to finish us off.

CHAPTER 24

"Kill them," Carson ordered his sharks.

The sharks flicked their tails, and they leapt out of the water, their teeth aimed straight at us. Our dolphins ducked under the surface, and Tristan turned to face the sharks. He aimed a stream of water at them that sent one of the sharks spinning off into the distance, but the other locked its eyes on the blood leaking from Tristan's arm. The shark aimed his teeth straight at Tristan.

I yanked on my dolphin's fin, and she responded to my urgency. She flicked her tail, and I used my magic to propel her faster through the water. We reached the shark a moment before it could clamp its teeth around the end of Tristan's tail.

Delphina rammed straight into the shark's side at the same time I blasted a stream of water at him. The shark spun, but it slowed and turned its angry eyes on me. Panic filled my chest, and I quickly commanded water to form like cannon balls in my palms. I shot the water outward, and one of the balls hit the end of the shark's nose. He shook his head, but never stopped swimming.

I readied for another attack, but I never had the chance to aim my magic. I felt the need to *protect* fill Delphina's thoughts, then she bucked me off her back and swam straight for the shark.

No! I tried to scream, but it was too late.

The shark's teeth sank into her side, and blood filled the water.

Agony twisted in my gut. Delphina's body sagged, and sobs racked my body as the shark drew away, exposing a large chunk of skin missing. Delphina—the dolphin I spent years caring for, who'd been my *friend*—was gone.

Tristan saw what happened, and I witnessed the anger mar his features as lightning flashed above the surface of the sea. He darted up behind the shark, then slammed his fist straight into its eyes. The shark reeled backward, blood leaking from its eye sockets. It shook its head, but in its now blinded state, it couldn't find its bearings.

Tristan grabbed me, and I held on to his back as he swam toward the surface. I looked around for Noah and Liana, but I didn't see them anywhere.

Waves thrashed us from side to side as I gulped a breath of air. My tone came out broken with the harrowing knowledge that Delphina's dead body floated only meters below us. "I lost Noah and Liana!"

"They're there," Tristan said, pointing toward the next wave.

My heart stalled when I saw my friends with their dolphins at the surface of the water. Carson rode on the back of the second shark and headed straight for them.

Liana and Noah shot streams of water at Carson, but nothing they did slowed him down. He was the master of these waters now, and we weren't strong enough to counteract his command of the sea.

"We have to overpower him," I insisted. If there was any hope of defeating him, it lied in Tristan's merfolk magic.

"Our magic is equally matched," Tristan said. "But if we can sneak up behind him—"

"Tristan!" I cried.

Carson's shark lunged at my friends. Instinctually, Tristan and I lifted our hands at the same time. Our power caused a massive wave to rise up and pull Carson and his shark away from our friends. The shark snapped its jaws, but its teeth met nothing but air. In the same moment, lightning flashed, and I caught sight of something blue slip out from beneath Carson's shirt. The stone he wore around his neck looked familiar.

I gasped. "Tristan, what did you say your necklace was made of?"

Tristan furrowed his brow, unsure where I was going with this. "Aquamarine. My people wear it for protection."

"Protection from *what*?" I asked.

"It's just an old wives' tale," he said. "It was meant to protect people at sea."

"I think that's what's protecting your magic," I realized. "Carson's weapon affects everyone in town—it's localized. Except it doesn't affect you, and it doesn't affect *him*. He's wearing the same stone around his neck—"

A wave crashed over us, and my words were drowned out by the sea. I was swept up in the current, and though I tried to hold tight to Tristan, my fingers slipped. The waves dragged me away, until I couldn't see him anymore.

Heart pounding, I fought against the current and dragged myself to the surface. I found myself at the peak of a wave that swelled at least fifty feet above the surrounding water. Rain pounded down on the surface of the ocean, making it hard to see.

I glanced around desperately for signs of life, until my eyes landed upon Carson in the water below me. He had his sights set on my friends, and though they fought back desperately, there was nothing they could do to stop the rage of his storm.

I was getting tired, and my limbs hurt from fighting the current. I gathered up the last bit of strength I had and commanded the water to propel me forward one last time. I reached the crest of the wave, and then suddenly, I was free-falling.

Lightning streaked across the sky, illuminating the ocean for the briefest of moments. My shadow crossed Carson's face, and his gaze darted upward. Another bolt of lightning illuminated the sky, and I caught the shock in his features.

I landed hard against Carson, knocking him off the back of his shark. We went tumbling into the water.

Carson punched the side of my face so hard I saw stars, but I tangled my hand in the collar of his shirt and reached for the stone hanging off his neck. My fingers curled around the string, and I pulled as hard as I could.

Carson opened his mouth, but only the beginning of a sonic scream ever came out, before I felt the snap of the necklace, and I held the stone in my hand. The red of his tail faded, and his bottom half morphed into legs covered by trousers once again.

Power surged through me stronger than the waves thrashing overhead. Last night when I told Noah I felt powerful, I hadn't realized why. I hadn't wanted to push my magic, but it hadn't occurred to me just how much magic I had at my disposal. I'd had Tristan's aquamarine stone in my pocket then, and just as I felt powerful then, I felt even more powerful now.

I inhaled a breath of water. It once felt like the air in my lungs, but now the connection went as deep as the blood in my veins. I was connected to the water, and it was connected to me. The ocean and I were one and the same. All the power of the ocean was mine.

Carson Ray had taken my power because he was afraid

of what I could do with it. I wouldn't let him silence me any longer.

I opened my mouth, and power unlike anything I'd felt before blasted out of me as I screamed. It shook the waters, reverberating to the depths of the sea.

My scream blasted Carson backward, but I wasn't done with him yet. I ordered the ocean to drag us both to the surface. I spotted my friends nearby, sagging against their dolphins. Carson Ray had beat the fight out of them with his storm, but I wasn't going to let him hurt them any longer.

Thunder cracked overhead, and water swirled around us at all angles. The waves carried me above Carson, and I stared down at him in distain.

"You never should've come back!" he shouted. "I compelled you to leave."

I recalled his last words after he'd taken my core. *I know people like you. You never leave well enough alone, but you will get on that plane, Miss Waters, and you will finish this.*

I smirked. "You told me to get on that plane. You never said I couldn't return. I guess you were right about me. I can't leave well enough alone—and I never leave my work unfinished."

Terror filled his eyes. "You don't know how to utilize your magic!"

"You think you control these waters and our city because you have magic? You stole our magic and left us powerless!" I screamed. "You lied to your people, and you used a weapon of war against them—all in the name of profit. Now, your weapon has become your weakness."

I called the water up from the sea, rising higher and higher, until the wave crested and blocked out the clouds completely. Carson shielded his face, like that might weaken the blow. I slammed my arms downward, and the wave echoed my command. Water crashed down on Carson, blasting him deep into the depths of the ocean.

Two sharks poked their heads of the water, as if awaiting instruction. One of them was still bleeding from the eyes.

"This man has stolen merfolk magic, and he threatens our waters. Go after him," I commanded. "And make sure he *never* makes it to shore."

The sharks ducked under water in pursuit of Carson Ray. I should've felt something when I sent them after him, but all I felt was relief.

Carson Ray would never steal anyone's magic again.

CHAPTER 25

The waves calmed, and the skies above us cleared. Sunlight shone down on us, and I spotted our sailboat off in the distance. I commanded the water to turn it upright and ordered the waves to carry it over to us.

My friends and I climbed onto the boat and fell onto our backs, panting. Tristan's tail turned back into legs, and his jeans were soaked. I clutched the aquamarine stone tightly in my hand.

The dolphins swam up to the edge of the boat. I felt their emotions with more clarity than ever before. They wanted to make sure we were all right. My heart dropped when I thought of Delphina and what she'd done for me, but I gave the dolphins a reassuring nod. Maybe I wasn't all right, but I was alive, and I was grateful for their help. The dolphins gave a few clicks, then swam off.

Noah turned his gaze toward mine, but he spoke through ragged breaths. "How did you do that?"

I pushed myself upright and showed him the stone. "Whatever Carson's doing to steal our magic, this counteracts it."

Tristan eyed the stone curiously. "This must be why my brothers didn't survive the storm when we came here. They didn't have a stone like me."

"That confirms that Carson's weapon affects all merfolk, regardless of where they came from," I said thoughtfully. "He mentioned something called a sea stone, but we have to figure out how it works, so that we can stop it and restore our people's right to their magic."

"We can't go back now," Noah insisted. "Carson wasn't running Blue Wave Energy alone. There were other people who knew what he was up to."

"Noah's right," Liana agreed. "If we go back now, they'll kill us for what we know."

I got to my feet and stared into the distance. All I could see now was the lighthouse on the horizon as the last of the shore disappeared. My hands curled around the boat's railing. "I sat around and let them throw me out of town, but I won't let them control me anymore. I won't let them take control of what rightfully belongs to our people. I'm going to find out how the sea stone works, and I'm going to stop it."

Tristan came up behind me and placed a hand on my shoulder. My body felt warm where he touched it. "If we're going to stop them, we'll need an army. Come to the Luna pod with me, and we'll gather support so that we can come back and help your people."

I gazed up at him, and for a moment I felt like I could follow those blue-green eyes anywhere. But it wouldn't be without consequences.

"I can't leave my parents and Christina behind," I insisted. "Liana's family doesn't even know where she is. They must be worried sick."

Noah approached me and placed his hand on mine. There was comfort in his touch that made me feel protected and safe, like I could believe anything he said. "Your families will worry, but at least out here you'll be *alive*. We have to do our best to help our people, and if that means turning to the Luna pod for help, then we have to make that journey."

"I'm in." Liana stood at the railing, looking out at the open ocean, before turning to me. "I don't want to leave, but we can't go back alone. Even with two aquamarine stones in our possession, we don't know how many stones Carson's people have, or how many people we'll be up against. We should visit the Luna pod with Tristan."

I kept my eyes on the horizon. I had no idea what I was getting myself into when I found Tristan washed up on the shores of Sea Haven Beach. The council had stolen my core, but I'd gotten it back. They'd locked Tristan up, and I'd freed him. Carson had come after us, and yet we were still standing on this boat. The Sea Haven Council had done everything to stop me from uncovering their sea of secrets, but I was only getting started.

"We'll go to the Luna pod and request their help," I agreed as stone-cold resolve washed over me. "Then we're going to uncover every secret the Sea Haven Council is hiding."

And no one—merfolk or otherwise—could stop us.

END OF BOOK ONE

Travel to the Luna pod in book two, *Rising Tides*.

ABOUT THE AUTHOR

Alicia Rades is a USA Today bestselling author of young adult and new adult paranormal fiction. When she's not dreaming up magical stories, she's either binge-watching paranormal TV shows, meditating, or spending time with her family. She has an unhealthy obsession with psychic characters and writes with a deck of tarot cards next to her computer.